"What *is* that thing?" Dora's father asked, his voice barely a whisper.

"I'll check it out." Theodore set the panic horn on the nightstand and looked under the bed.

"Be careful . . . ," Charlie warned.

"Hey. Relax. It's *me*."

Three black tentacles exploded from the front of the oozing creature and snaked wetly around Theodore's face.

"It's got me!" he shrieked.

Then—with one quick, strong tug—the Darkling yanked Theodore under the bed and into its drooling, toothy mouth. . . .

NIGHTMARE ACADEMY
MONSTER MADNESS

BOOK 2

~~~

by DEAN LOREY

Illustrations by
BRANDON DORMAN

HARPER
An Imprint of HarperCollinsPublishers

Nightmare Academy, Book Two: Monster Madness

Text copyright © 2008 by Dean Lorey

Illustrations copyright © 2008 by Brandon Dorman

www.harpercollinschildrens.com

Library of Congress Cataloging-in-Publication Data

Lorey, Dean.

Monster madness / by Dean Lorey ; illustrations by Brandon
Dorman. —1st ed.

p.   cm. — (Nightmare Academy ; #2)

Summary: Thirteen-year-old Charlie Benjamin and his fellow
students at the Nightmare Academy try to stop the four Named
Lords of the Nether from coming to Earth and summoning an
even more deadly creature called the Fifth.

ISBN 978-0-06-134047-5

[1. Monsters—Fiction. 2. Schools—Fiction. 3. Friendship—
Fiction. 4. Fantasy.] I. Dorman, Brandon, ill. II. Title.

PZ7.L88638Mo 2008   2008016219

[Fic]—dc22   CIP

                                                          AC

Typography by Ray W. Shappell

09 10 11 12 13 LP/CW 10 9 8 7 6 5 4 3 2 1

❖

First paperback edition, 2009

To my folks, Craig and Marilyn.

You can't choose your parents . . .

so I guess I just got lucky.

I love you both.

Contents

PART
· I ·

ESCAPE FROM
THE NETHER

· CHAPTER ONE ·
DORA'S DARKLING

Final exams don't normally end in death, but Charlie Benjamin wasn't normal, and neither was the final exam he and his friends were about to take.

"Monsters, watch out!" Theodore exclaimed as he, Charlie, and Violet gathered their gear on the deck of the pirate ship at the very top of the Nightmare Academy. "Soon as this exam's over, we're gonna be Noobs no more!"

In the six months they'd been training, the gigantic banyan tree that held the Academy in its mighty branches had come to feel like home—Charlie knew every weathered plank of every wrecked boat nestled there. It had been a lot of work, of course. He'd lost count of the numerous bites and scratches he'd received from the Class-1 monsters in Beginning Banishing, and having to continually summon your deepest, darkest fears to open portals in Neophyte Nethermancy was no picnic, either.

But none of that mattered, really.

For every bad time, there were three good ones—swimming in the clear, warm ocean with Violet and Theodore; playing hide-and-seek in the Academy's crazy web of catwalks, boats, and branches; eating wild plums with sweet purple juice dripping down their chins.

It had been heaven . . . and it had all led to this moment.

"That final exam is toast!" Theodore shouted. "You just let me at those monsters and I will show you the true meaning of the words *pest control*! I am a walking, talking can of Raid!"

"Well, you're definitely as tall and skinny as one," Violet said with a laugh.

"And just as deadly," Theodore shot back. "I am extra-strength Raid—do not point at face, do not use near open flame, wash hands after use!"

"I'm just glad the day is finally here," Charlie said, grinning. "I feel like we've been Noobs forever."

"Because we have!" Theodore seemed as if he were in actual physical pain at the thought. "I mean, come on, we should have been promoted to Addy, like, forever ago! After all, who rescued your mom and dad from the lair of Barakkas and Verminion?"

"Us."

"You're dang right, *us*, and on only our second day at the Academy! We are the A-Team! The Nether Squad! The Monster Mashers!"

"Okay, okay, calm down." Charlie was laughing now. "Don't worry, we're gonna get plenty of opportunity to strut our stuff tonight."

"You can say that again! I'll tell you this much, I am seriously RTR!"

"Ready to roll?" Violet asked.

"No, that would be utterly ridiculous." Theodore hated it whenever anyone guessed the meanings of his initials before he explained them. "It stands for . . ." He seemed to search for an answer—then his eyes lit up. "Really Truly Righteous!"

"You just made that up!"

But before Theodore could respond, a fiery purple portal snapped open next to them. Rex, Tabitha, and Pinch stepped through.

"Howdy, my eager little Noobs," Rex said in his thick Texas drawl, a wide grin plastered across his tanned face. He was dressed in his usual outfit of faded jeans, worn boots, and a crisp cowboy hat. A lasso was loosely looped at his hip, accompanied by a gleaming short sword. "You ready for your big final?"

"More than ready," Charlie replied. "I feel like we've been ready for forever."

"Then let's get it done. Like my daddy always said—failure is not an option."

"We are going to destroy that final!" Theodore blurted. "Utterly annihilate it! Spank it on its—"

"Asinine," Pinch interrupted, shaking his head. "All this boastfulness is just asinine."

"Nothing wrong with a little confidence, Pinch," Tabitha said, her green eyes sparkling as brilliantly as the jewels that decorated her short, red hair. "You were that eager once. Remember?"

"I try not to," Pinch replied with a sigh. "Let's just get on with it, shall we? The sooner we start, the sooner we finish, and I'd prefer not to spend my entire evening waiting for these Noobs to bumble their way to becoming Addys—that is, assuming they succeed."

"We will," Violet said, smiling. "Failure is not an option."

"I wonder where I've heard *that* before . . . ," Pinch muttered.

"Dunno," Rex replied. "From someone very wise, I suspect. And very handsome. And clever. And—"

Tabitha held up a finger to his lips, silencing him. "Why don't we just go get those monsters, huh?"

With a wave of her hand, she opened a portal to the Nether.

The first thing Charlie noticed when he stepped back to Earth was the smell: rot. It came from the murky water of a leaf-filled swimming pool in a courtyard surrounded by several small, run-down bungalows. Many of them were boarded up, as unused as the broken Big Wheel that lay overturned on the weedy lawn. The light from the cloud-covered moon was thin and fleeting.

"We're looking for bungalow C," Pinch said, peering into the darkness. "Ah, there it is."

He pointed to a weathered green bungalow. The yellow lamp on the wall next to the front door sputtered fitfully, casting dim, uncertain light.

"Looks kind of spooky," Violet said.

"Duh!" Theodore shot back. "That's 'cause it's full of monsters. Hello?"

"Can I punch him?"

Charlie shook his head. "He's too fragile. You might break him."

"Fragile!" Theodore roared. "Did I just have a mental spasm, or did you say the *girl* might break me? Because that's seriously—"

"Let's continue, shall we?" Pinch interrupted with a

roll of the eyes. "This bungalow is your target and here is your panic horn." He handed Theodore a red airhorn, which looked like an aerosol spray can with a funnel at one end. "If you press the button, we will immediately come to your aid, but remember—"

Theodore pressed the button.

The horn blared so loudly that Charlie leaped backward into Violet, accidentally elbowing her in the face. "Oww!" she yelped.

"Sorry."

"*Never* do that again!" Pinch commanded, clutching his heart as dogs barked angrily throughout the neighborhood. "It is to be used only in case of extreme emergency!"

"*No problemo,*" Theodore said. "Just wanted to test it out, is all—make sure it worked. Anyone with any smarts knows to COYG—check out your gear. That's rule *numero uno*, which is Spanish for—"

"I know what it's for!" Pinch snapped. He closed his eyes and stroked his beard to calm himself before continuing. "Remember, you are to use the panic horn only if absolutely necessary, because if you force us to step in and help you on your final exam, you will fail. To succeed, you must always expect—"

"A pig in a tutu?" Rex asked.

"No," Pinch replied, glaring at him. "Not a pig in

a tutu. You must always expect—"

"A juggling otter?"

"The unexpected!" Pinch snapped back.

"Hmm. Interesting. I didn't expect you to say that." Rex shot Charlie a friendly wink, and it was everything Charlie could do to keep from laughing.

Tabitha shook her head, clearly getting annoyed. "Can we just stop this nonsense so the kids can take their exam already?"

"Don't you just love how she looks when she gets huffy?" Rex said with a grin. "Them little chipmunk cheeks pop out, and she gets that cute little crinkle above her nose."

"Chipmunk cheeks!"

"Oooh! See how mad she's pretending to be now? I call that her 'I'm in love with Rex but tryin' hard not to show it' face."

Tabitha's jaw dropped. She turned to the kids with as much dignity as she could muster. "Your final exam begins now. A frightened little girl named Dora has been portaling monsters into our world during her nightmares. She and her father have absolutely no idea what's going on. Their bungalow is infested, which means you need to find a way inside, identify the monsters there, and get rid of them. You have one hour."

"Easy-peasy mac and cheesy," Theodore replied. He turned to Charlie. "Am I right or am I right?"

"I have absolutely no idea what you just said, but here's what I was thinking: We sneak around to the back of the building and look in through the windows. You know, secretly inspect the place, see what we're dealing with. Then—"

"Or we could just do this."

Theodore rang the doorbell.

Rex, Tabitha, and Pinch barely managed to scramble out of view before the door swung open to reveal a large man holding a large baseball bat in the hairy knuckles of his thick, sausagelike fingers.

"What do you want?" the man asked. His bat gleamed dully in the light of the wall lamp.

"Um," Charlie replied, startled. "Well, see, we were sent here by the Nightmare Academy to investigate a suspected portaling of Nethercreatures by your daughter, Dora."

"Huh?" the man said, leaning toward them.

"I see I'm not explaining myself very well." Charlie backed up, his voice rising nervously. "What I mean is—"

"Look here, pal," Theodore interrupted, getting right in the large man's face. "You are IWM. Know what that means? Infested with monsters. We're here to get rid of 'em."

The large man stared down at him, then slammed the door.

"Well, that's just great!" Charlie exclaimed. "Thanks, Theodore."

"That wasn't my fault! I wasn't the one fumbling around, talking about 'what I mean is . . . what I intend to say is . . . blah, blah, blabbety, blah, blah.'"

"I had a plan, and if you hadn't got in the way, we'd probably be inside the house right now! You don't just go and ring the doorbell with no warning!"

Without warning, Violet rang the doorbell.

"What are you doing?" Charlie said, aghast.

"I'll handle this."

The door opened and the same large man stood there with the same large bat. He glared at her.

"I know how you're feeling," Violet said soothingly. "You're scared. Something's happening inside your house—something you don't understand—and you want to protect yourself and your family, but you don't know how or from what. That's why you carry around that bat, isn't it?"

The man's eyes narrowed but he said nothing.

"It was the same way in my house," Violet continued. "I used to have terrible nightmares, and my parents would hear screams and growls coming from my bedroom—horrible, horrible sounds—but they never knew what was causing them. They only knew that something was wrong and that I was in trouble. Then one day some people showed up and offered to help." She smiled warmly. "We're those people. And we're here to help. My name's Violet."

She stuck out her hand. The man looked at it for a long time.

"Name's Barry," he said finally, taking her hand in his. "Boy, am I glad you're here."

Dora was eight years old.

Her face was round and pale and her eyes, which hung like twin moons below straight, black hair, were dark and haunted. "Do you know what's been happening to me?" she whispered.

"It's been insane around here," her father added. "Howls and crashes, furniture busted, carpet all ripped up—but only at night."

"How long has it been going on?" Charlie asked, glancing around at the dimly lit bungalow. The wallpaper had pictures of fruit on it that might once have looked cheerful, but now looked old and rotten. A pot of SpaghettiOs bubbled on the ancient stove.

"I guess it all started when her mama passed,"

Dora's father said with a sigh. "That was, what, a year ago?"

"I'm so sorry." Violet reached out and stroked Dora's hair. "I lost my mother a long time ago, too."

"You did?"

Violet nodded. "It was the worst thing that ever happened to me. I had terrible nightmares for months after." She smiled gently. "What about you?"

Dora nodded. "*Terrible* ones."

The lights flickered in the already dim living room. Charlie and his friends glanced knowingly at one another.

"So . . . can you help us?" Dora's father asked, turning to Charlie.

"I think so. Here's what's been going on. Some kids have what's called 'the Gift'—although sometimes it feels more like a curse. When kids with the Gift have nightmares, they open portals to the Netherworld, where monsters live. Sometimes those monsters come through the portals and into our world, where they cause all kinds of problems—just like the ones you've been having."

"You're serious, huh?" Dora's father said. "Portals? Monsters?"

Charlie nodded. "I think you've got a Gremlin infestation. That's why the power is so funny in here:

They like to chew on electric cables."

The large man eyed him skeptically. "Prove it."

Dora's room was darker than the rest of the house, and that was with all the lights on. Stepping inside was like stepping into a tomb. Stuffed animals were scattered across her bed like sentries, a crystal unicorn collection sat on a small shelf, and night-lights were plugged into every available outlet, but no amount of light could overcome the miserable gloom.

"This is my bedroom," Dora said softly. Charlie noticed that she was reluctant to enter. He didn't blame her.

"No worries, kid," Theodore exclaimed. "The A-Team is here. We'll take care of this in a jiffy."

Charlie crossed to the middle of the room. "All right, here we go." He extended his right hand, closed his eyes, and began to open a portal.

Even under the best of circumstances, portaling was an incredibly difficult job. You had to identify your most personal fear, summon it, and then focus it like a laser on a specific location in your mind's eye—only then could you open up a portal to the exact place you'd imagined. It was a bit like juggling spaghetti while doing the tango. But in the six months that Charlie had been practicing the art of Nethermancy at the Nightmare Academy, it had gotten much easier and he was now able to open portals with remarkable speed.

Almost immediately, electric purple flame began to dance across him, and a six-foot-wide portal popped open, also ringed with purple fire. Through it, everyone could see the bluish, rocky plains of the 1st ring of the Nether. It was flat and featureless, except for a strange object that sat improbably on the gritty sand—

A tall, metal cabinet with a simple handle.

"What's that for?" Violet asked.

"You'll see." Charlie stepped through the portal.

Even though he'd done it hundreds of times, entering the Nether was still an odd and disorienting experience. All the angles seemed slightly wrong somehow, and he was conscious of unusual movement around him, subtle things he'd learned to identify with experience—the eerie drift of a ghost floating by or the slight buckle of a Netherworm tunneling through the sand beneath his feet.

He glanced around to make sure no creatures were lying in wait, then lifted the handle on the cabinet. It released with a satisfying *click*, and Charlie opened the door to reveal a treasure trove of Banishing gear: tracking devices and spare rapiers; bags of flour for crippling Netherbats; flashlights for herding Ectobogs; traps for capturing Snarks; and various elixirs to heal a wound, counteract poison, or stop the spread of disease from a monster's bite. It was everything a Banisher needed for a confrontation with even the wildest of wildlife from the Nether.

"No *way*!" Theodore exclaimed. "When did you put all this together?"

"Been working on it." Charlie shrugged, although he was secretly incredibly proud of himself. "I figured, why carry around the million different things you might need during a Banishing? Why not just stow it all in the Nether, where it's only a portal away?"

"Genius. Pure genius."

"I gotta tell you," Violet added, "that's pretty amazing."

"And check this out," Charlie said happily, pleased by their praise. He reached into the back of the cabinet and pulled out a heavy, metal object. It was the size and shape of a toaster and had numerous switches and lights on it.

"What's that crazy-looking thing?" Theodore asked.

"Watch." Charlie stepped back into the bedroom. With a wave of his hand, he closed the portal behind him and then set the metal contraption on the floor next to the bed. He flipped a switch. The strange device began to hum as the lights on it glowed.

"It's actually just a modified car battery," Charlie explained. "It doesn't last as long as a regular one, but it puts out a ton more juice."

"It's a Gremlin attractor!" Violet exclaimed.

Charlie nodded. "The little pests can't resist this thing. Just watch. It won't take long for those electricity junkies to show up."

It didn't.

Dora's closet door swung open with a creak, and a monkeylike creature with orange fur, a long tail, and a wide jaw scrambled through. The electricity inside the battery drew the Gremlin like a magnet—it didn't even seem to notice the humans.

"That thing was living in my *closet*?" Dora asked incredulously.

"Yup," Charlie answered. "And I bet it's not the only one around."

It wasn't.

Moments later, a second Gremlin dropped into the room through an air vent in the ceiling, and a third came running in from the hallway, brushing past Dora's father as it did. All three creatures crowded around the battery and began gnawing at it with their thick teeth, trying to get to the delicious electricity coursing inside.

"Sweet!" Theodore exclaimed. "That looks like all

of them, so I'll just go ahead and banish them back to the Nether real quick . . ."

He stepped toward the creatures, but Charlie put out a hand to stop him.

"What?"

"Why don't you let the Banisher do the banishing?" Charlie nodded to Violet.

"Oh, come on," Theodore moaned. "I can do it. They're just Gremlins—they're the trash of the Nether!"

"I know you can do it, but she can do it much better, just like you can portal way better than she can."

"Portaling is for sissies," Theodore grumbled. Even after six months of training, he still regretted not having been picked as a Banisher by the Trout of Truth, but he stepped aside to let Violet approach. The old, pitted dagger she kept between her belt and her jeans glowed a dim electric blue as she neared the Nethercreatures.

One by one, they stopped chewing on the battery and took notice of her and her glowing blade.

"Hi, little fellas," she said. Then, with truly magnificent speed, she snatched two of them up by the scruff of the neck. They shrieked furiously, trying to snap at her with their filthy mouths. "Bite me and I'll bite you back," she threatened, then nodded to the remaining

Gremlin by the battery. "Theodore, you wanna help me out and grab that last one?"

"Sure thing!"

As he reached for the creature, a black tentacle suddenly shot out from underneath Dora's bed. It snatched the Gremlin and yanked it into the darkness.

"What was that?" Charlie yelled.

The captured Gremlin started squealing as if in terrible pain, then went suddenly, ominously silent.

Next came the crunching sounds.

"I think I'm gonna be sick," Dora said, clutching her stomach. "Do something . . ."

But, before anyone could, two more tentacles shot out, snatched the remaining Gremlins right out of Violet's hands, and yanked them into the darkness under the bed.

More squealing. More crunching sounds.

"What *is* that thing?" Dora's father asked, his voice barely a whisper.

"I'll check it out." Theodore set the panic horn on the nightstand and looked under the bed.

"Be careful . . . ," Charlie warned.

"Hey. Relax. It's *me*."

A heaving mass of flesh pulsed softly in the shadows, black and shiny as motor oil, with two red eyes and an irregular mouth full of twisty, sharp teeth. As the thing finished chewing the last of the Gremlins, its body expanded until its slick back touched the bottom of the box spring.

"Wow!" Theodore exclaimed. "She's got a Darkling! Looks like a Class 2!"

Three black tentacles exploded from the front of the oozing creature and snaked wetly around Theodore's face.

"It's got me!" he shrieked.

Then—with one quick, strong tug—the Darkling yanked Theodore under the bed and into its drooling, toothy mouth. . . .

CHAPTER TWO

ATTACK OF THE DANGEROOS

"Honk the panic horn! Honk the panic horn!" Theodore screamed as the Darkling's glistening forest of teeth opened wide to swallow him.

"No, we got ya!" Charlie yelled as he and Violet leaped on Theodore's legs, trying to pull him away from the grip of those terrible black tentacles—but to no avail. Charlie was amazed by how strong the filthy thing was.

"It's not working!" Theodore screeched. He could feel wet pieces of Gremlin dangling on his face as they hung from the teeth of the vicious creature. "Just honk the panic horn!"

"If we honk it, we fail the exam!" Violet said.

"If you don't honk it, I fail my life!"

Charlie turned to Dora and her father. "Pull the

bed away from the Darkling—expose it to the light!"

The large man looked worried. "But what if it bites—"

"Just pull it!" Theodore shrieked, his voice spiraling to crazy, girlish heights.

Dora and her father grabbed hold of the bed and yanked it to the side, uncovering the Darkling beneath. As soon as the light from the room touched it, the creature howled in pain and let Theodore go, sending Charlie and Violet flying backward. It quickly retreated into the familiar shadows under the bed, where it pulsated quietly in the darkness.

There was silence then as all of them caught their breath. Finally, Theodore spoke:

"When I say honk the panic horn . . . *you honk the panic horn, you got me?*"

"Everything was under control," Charlie replied. "The Darkling wanted the darkness more than it wanted you. Don't worry, we wouldn't have let it eat you."

"Well, that's comforting! Why don't you climb under the bed and give it a good-night kiss? Don't worry, I won't let it eat *you*."

"And I don't want it to eat my *daughter*," Dora's father said. "But it's still under her bed. How are you gonna get rid of it?"

"Not sure," Violet replied. "I know that sunlight

kills them—they absorb light, which is why it's so incredibly gloomy in here, but they can't absorb that much light. Unfortunately, it's nighttime right now."

"We could wait till morning," Theodore suggested.

"And fail the exam? We have less than an hour before our time's up, and it's still nine more hours till sunup."

"Not in China," Charlie said, turning to them. "It's on the other side of the Earth, so it's already daytime there."

"So what?" Theodore replied. "We can't exactly bring the Darkling to China."

"No, but we *can* bring China to the Darkling—or at least its sun. That is, if we work together."

Theodore thought about that for a second, and then a wide grin broke out across his face. "You, sir, are a supergenius."

After a minute of struggling, Theodore finally managed to open a portal to the 1st Ring of the Nether.

"Good job," Violet said.

The skinny boy flushed with pride. "Ah, I'm still nowhere near as fast as portal master over there." He nodded to Charlie. "After all, he *is* the DT."

The DT.

The Double-Threat.

Charlie hated the term. He never asked to be a Double-Threat (or a DT as Theodore insisted on calling him)—he was just born that way. As far as Charlie was concerned, the ability to Banish *and* Nethermance was more of a curse than a blessing. Everyone else with the Gift could do only one or the other, and it made him crazy to be so different from them. In fact, the Headmaster of the Nightmare Academy was the only other Double-Threat in existence, which made him feel like that much more of a freak.

"I may be a little bit quicker at opening portals," Charlie replied, somewhat defensively, "but it's still gonna take both of us to do this thing—no one can open more than one portal at the same time."

"Duh," Theodore said. "Tell me something I *don't* know. I opened mine—now you open yours."

"Okay, get ready. Here we go." Charlie stepped through Theodore's portal and into the Nether. He extended his hand and closed his eyes. Moments later, purple flame crackled across him, and he opened up a portal that looked out on top of the Great Wall of China. Camera-wielding tourists screamed and stumbled backward, startled by the otherworldly sight.

Brilliant sunlight flooded through Charlie's portal—illuminating the rocky landscape of the 1st ring of the Nether—then continued on through

Theodore's portal and into Dora's small room beyond, filling it with light.

The Darkling instantly recoiled farther under the bed, desperately seeking protection in the shadows.

"Pull the mattress off!" Charlie yelled. "Expose it to the sun!"

Violet grabbed one side of the worn mattress as Dora's father grabbed the other.

"On three," she said. "One . . . two . . ."

They yanked the mattress off the bed, allowing the sunlight to blast the cowering Darkling below. The monster howled in agony as its skin sizzled and popped like the bubbles on a cheese pizza. Within moments, it liquefied into an oily pool that drained away through the floorboards.

Everyone stared in amazement.

"Is it . . . ?" Dora's father asked.

"Yeah," Charlie replied. "It's dead. Great job, everyone." He waved his hand and dismissed the portal to China. The blazing sunlight disappeared as if turned off by a switch.

"Wow!" Dora said, looking around. "I can't believe it. It's so bright in here now!"

"Get rid of a Darkling, get rid of the darkness," Charlie said with a grin as he stepped through Theodore's portal and back into Dora's bedroom.

"Plus," Theodore added, "now that the Gremlins are toast, you can start making toast again—your electricity shouldn't be so funky now that they're gone. And we did it all on our own! Congratulations, Addys!"

But, before they could celebrate, a reeking, green-furred creature the size of a refrigerator leaped through Theodore's still-open portal and landed on the hardwood floor of the bedroom with a loud crash. It stood upright, like a giant kangaroo, and had two thick, powerful legs and a wide pouch on its expansive belly. It howled obscenely as syrupy drool dripped from its long front fangs.

"What is that?" Violet said, startled.

Suddenly, the beast snatched her with its two strong forepaws, lifted her high into the air, and stuffed her, screaming, into its large front pouch. It turned and leaped back through Theodore's portal, escaping into the Nether beyond.

"It's got her!" Charlie shouted. "Theodore, honk the panic horn!"

"Oh, sure—when *I* almost get eaten, it's all 'we got you, Theodore—don't honk the panic horn,' but when Violet gets snatched, suddenly the world's gonna end!"

"Hurry! It's getting away! Just honk the stupid horn already!"

"Fine." Theodore grabbed it from the nightstand.

"But I just want to point out that compared to Banishers, Nethermancers are second-class citizens. We're Dopey to their Snow White. We're—"

"*JUST HONK THE HORN!*"

"*OKAY!*"

Theodore honked the panic horn.

Moments later, Rex came bursting through the bedroom door, followed by Pinch and Tabitha.

"What's going on?" she shouted.

"One of those things grabbed Violet!" Charlie pointed to a monstrous herd of the creatures as they neared the open portal.

Rex's eyes narrowed. "Son of a gun: Dangeroos. Class 4's by the look of their tails."

"The correct term is *Netherleapers*," Pinch said with a sniff.

"Aw, c'mon, Pinch, not every dang creature can start with *Nether*. Netherleapers, Netherstalkers, Netherbats—when's the madness gonna end?"

"Well, don't yell at me," Pinch replied. "I didn't name them—the Nightmare Division did."

"They've got Violet!" Charlie shouted. "Can we please *do* something!"

"Sure, kid," Rex said. "Follow me. Everyone else, stay here." He leaped through the portal and onto the 1st Ring.

The horrific stink of the approaching Dangeroos made Charlie's eyes water. "They look hungry," he said, backing away.

"Yeah," Rex replied. "There's nothing a Dangeroo likes more than chowin' down on a nice, tasty McHuman burger."

Charlie went pale. "What's gonna happen to Violet?"

"Aw, don't worry—they like to tenderize their food first. Your basic Dangeroo'll stick ya in their pouch and hop around a bit before eating ya. Heck, she's prolly got a good five minutes before the one that took her starts to feed."

"Starts to feed . . ." Charlie felt nauseous.

"Now, get ready." Rex unlooped his lasso. It glowed a brilliant blue. "I think I see our ride. Hold on to my waist. Hold tight."

Charlie did as he was told just as Rex lashed out with his lasso. It arrowed away from him like a lightning bolt, and the noose at the end settled around the neck of the nearest Dangeroo—a particularly tall one whose right eye glowed a milky, sightless white.

"Gotcha!"

The Dangeroo bolted into the air, and Rex and Charlie were yanked after it like a tin can tied to a car bumper. The acceleration nearly knocked the wind out of them. As they soared up, Charlie was startled to see how high they were—the 1st Ring of the Nether stretched out beneath them like a blue picnic blanket. His eyes were suddenly drawn to brilliant purple flashes that winked on and off like fireflies.

Portals, he realized with astonishment. *Those purple flashes are portals created by kids having nightmares!*

"Hang on!" Rex yelled as the Dangeroo arced back down toward the ground with sickening speed. "This is the tricky part!"

Charlie clamped his arms around Rex's waist as Rex shimmied along the rope until he was close enough to the Dangeroo to be able to grab on to its stinking, hairy back. The monster finished its descent and slammed into the hard earth, absorbing the impact in its piston-like legs. Then it sprang forward once again, rocketing high into the air. As it did, Rex yanked on the fiery blue lasso, causing the Dangeroo to gasp for breath.

"What are you doing?" Charlie shouted.

"Gotta break it—show it who's boss, same way you'd tame a wild horse."

The Dangeroo, straining against the noose, slammed back into the ground with less grace this time. It tumbled forward and then regained its footing. Charlie struggled to hold on as Rex pulled hard on the rope.

"Give it up, ya filthy thing! You ain't gonna win this one!"

The lasso sizzled against the monster's neck, and Charlie could smell burning hair. The Dangeroo bucked, trying to throw them off, but Rex wasn't having any of it.

"You give?" he shouted.

The Dangeroo growled and, craning its neck around, snapped at the cowboy, trying to bite his leg. Rex kicked it in the nose and pulled even tighter on the rope.

"I said, *do you give?*"

Finally, the creature stopped fighting.

"There," Rex said, using his forearm to wipe a glistening sheen of sweat from his brow. "Now—which way was Violet headed?"

Charlie pointed.

"Then let's go get her! Hi-yah!" Rex kicked the Dangeroo hard in the ribs.

The monster shot into the air like a cannonball and soared after the one that had kidnapped Violet. Charlie's cheeks rippled and his breath caught in his chest as the monster rocketed up into the sky, followed by a stomach-churning weightlessness as it descended. The distance between the two beasts narrowed until finally they were side by side.

"Violet!" Charlie yelled. "Are you okay?"

Violet managed to worm her head out of the suffocating fold of skin on the monster's belly. "Charlie! What do I do?"

"Just hold tight! We're here to rescue you!"

"Great! How?"

Charlie realized that he didn't have a clue.

"Now, get ready, kid," Rex said. "Soon as I release this lasso, the Dangeroo's gonna buck us off."

"What do you mean? We're just gonna fall?"

"Of course not! What kinda stupid plan is that?" Rex rolled his eyes. "No, when we get bucked, we're gonna leap out onto the Dangeroo that's got Violet."

"But what if we miss? It's a nearly impossible jump!"

"Which is why it's perfect for a Banisher! Nethermancers use fear to open their portals, but us Banishers use good, old-fashioned *courage* to do our job. Crazy thing is, you can only be courageous in the face of something that scares the tar outa you, so the scarier the challenge, the stronger we get when doing it!"

And with that he loosed the lasso from around their Dangeroo's neck, and he and Charlie leaped out into the air. They hurtled down as Violet's Dangeroo shot up beside them, so close that Charlie could feel the monster's coarse hair brush his cheek. As they passed,

Rex threw his lasso around the monster's neck. It yanked them upward with such force that Charlie barely managed to hang on to Rex's leather belt.

"Hey! Don't pull my pants off, kid!"

"I'm not trying to, but I'm losing my grip!"

"Well, hang on! I gotta wrestle this critter to the ground."

With Charlie in tow, Rex climbed along the lasso to the Dangeroo's back and tightened the noose. The monster howled and snapped, but Rex only grew more determined.

"You ain't gonna win this one, sunshine!"

Finally, it stopped trying to bite him, and Charlie could actually see some of the fight go out of its eyes.

"It's giving up!"

"Starting to," Rex replied, "but we ain't there yet. You okay, Violet?"

"Can't . . . breathe . . . ," she gasped, her voice muffled. The pouch had closed tightly over her head, and Charlie could see the outline of her body writhing inside.

"Don't worry!" Charlie yelled. "We'll get you out of there in just a second—we got it all under control!"

Suddenly, they heard a piercing shriek from somewhere high up above. Charlie looked behind him to see a giant Netherbat swooping down out of the churning sky, its large leather wings flapping furiously.

"Oh, no," Rex moaned as the monstrous flying creature snatched the Dangeroo by the head with its filthy talons. The Dangeroo jerked and spasmed wildly as the bat carried it, and its unfortunate passengers, high into the air.

"Hey, kid!" Rex shouted. "Don't you *ever* say 'we got it all under control' until *we got it all under control*!"

"Sorry," Charlie replied, then drew his glowing blue rapier.

"What the heck is that for?"

"Violet's suffocating. We gotta do something."

"Like what? We're a mile off the ground!"

It was true. The Netherbat had carried them so high that Charlie could now see all five Rings of the Nether spread out below them like the world's scariest board game.

"Didn't you just tell me an impossible plan is the perfect kind of plan for a Banisher?" Charlie asked.

"Yeah, but kid—I was exaggerating!"

"Sorry, didn't hear that last part."

With one mighty swipe of his rapier, Charlie sliced off the bat's talons. The winged creature shrieked in pain as the Dangeroo—with Charlie, Rex and Violet on board—plummeted down toward the distant rocks below.

CHAPTER THREE

AN EVIL PLOT

C harlie heard a keen whistling sound as the wind whipped past his face. The hard landscape of the Nether rose up to meet them with astonishing speed, and he knew that if they hit it their bodies were going to be splattered across the 1st Ring.

"If you got a plan, kid," Rex shouted, "now would be a heckuva good time to put it into action!"

Charlie *did* have a plan—but it was a desperate one.

He closed his eyes, extended his right hand, and began to summon a portal. Purple fire raced across him. Just as he, Rex, and Violet were about to slam into the lifeless, moonlike surface, a portal snapped open beneath them. They fell through it to land in the murky swimming pool in front of Dora's bungalow with a great explosion of water.

The Dangeroo took the brunt of the impact, and Charlie felt its ribcage snap like the plastic bristles of an old comb. The displaced water crashed down on top of them, battering them as they thrashed around in the deep end of the cloudy, green pool. Only one thought raced through Charlie's mind:

Violet.

Is she alive? Did she survive the impact?

He frantically swam underneath the Dangeroo and tried to open its front pouch to free her, but all the muscles on the creature's belly had spasmed from the trauma of the fall. The pouch was sealed as tightly as a bank vault. He braced his legs against the unmoving beast's chest and pulled on the pouch's opening with all his might, but it was hopeless.

Violet.

Please be alive. . . .

Suddenly, a glowing blue blade pierced the leather skin of the Dangeroo's stomach, and Charlie realized that Violet was using her dagger to cut her way out of her fleshy prison. The water in the pool clouded with black ichor as the creature bled from the wound, but Violet's weapon shined through the murk like a beacon. Charlie reached forward, grabbed her by the arm, and pulled her through the slit in the beast's pouch. Then they shot up to the surface, where they both breathed deeply of the cool, delicious night air.

"Thanks," Violet said, her arm still locked around Charlie's. "I could have died."

"Aw, it was nothing," he replied, blushing. "I mean, not that you being alive is nothing. That's definitely *something*. I just meant—"

"There you are!"

Charlie turned to see Theodore running toward them from the apartment complex, followed by Tabitha, Pinch, Dora, and her father. Theodore leaped up and down joyfully.

"I knew you'd survive! Excellent! Never a doubt!"

"Yeah, we survived," Rex said as he climbed out of the pool. "But it got pretty dicey there for a while."

"And the monster?" Dora asked nervously.

"Dead," Charlie said, as he and Violet grabbed on to Rex's outstretched hands. The cowboy pulled them from the water. "I think the fall killed it."

Suddenly, the wounded—but clearly alive—Dangeroo shot out of the inky murk in a foul spray. It landed at the edge of the pool, scrabbled frantically on the slick tiles, and then lost its footing and slipped back into the black depths with a howl. Before it could make another escape attempt, Tabitha quickly opened a large portal at the very bottom of the pool. The water rushed through the gateway and, like the flushing of some giant toilet, sucked the Dangeroo back into the Nether.

With a quick wave of Tabitha's hand, the portal disappeared and the empty pool was still.

"*Now* it's dead," Rex said. "Or at least gone." He turned to Charlie. "Kid, from now on, you're forbidden from saying anything even remotely like 'the fall killed it,' 'we've got it all under control,' or 'everything's all right'—you got me?"

"Got you."

Rex shot him a playful wink as Violet kneeled down in front of Dora.

"Are you okay?" the older girl asked. "You still frightened about going back into your bedroom?"

"A little. What if I have another nightmare?"

"Don't you worry," her father replied. "I'm here. And now that I know what's going on, I won't let them get you again." He tapped his baseball bat in his meaty palm.

"And we'll be checking in on you," Violet added, stroking the girl's silken hair. "Someday soon, you'll be old enough for training at the Academy. Would you like that?"

Dora nodded. "I want to be just like all of you."

"You hang in there and someday you will be."

"Good."

Charlie wondered what tortured path the little girl's

Gift would eventually lead her down. Would she be a Banisher and use her skills to fight the monsters of her nightmares? Or would she be a Nethermancer and summon up her greatest fears to open portals for traveling through the terrible ferocity of the Nether?

Either way, he empathized with her. He knew how brutally difficult it was to be young and afraid of what horrors you might conjure, late at night, alone in the dark. . . .

"Well, I think we've had enough drama for one day," Tabitha said with a smile. She turned to Charlie and his friends. "Don't you agree . . . , Addys?"

"Theodore Dagget—Addy!" the skinny boy exclaimed. "That's my name—keep sayin' it, it'll still be the same!"

"Not so fast," Pinch said. "Technically speaking, you didn't pass the exam: You used the panic horn."

"Well, yeah," Charlie replied, "because Violet was dying."

"Even so, it was a clear violation of the rules. A true Addy would have been able to recover from the situation without our help."

"Aw, c'mon!" Rex roared. "Don't be ridiculous. The test is set up to see if kids can handle Banishing a couple Class 1 critters—not Class 4's! I mean, what the heck were Class 4's doing on the 1st Ring, anyway?"

"That's entirely beside the point."

"No," Tabitha said. "Rex is right. That *is* the point—the only one that matters, anyway. Why were those Class 4's there? I've never seen that before."

"Not only that," Charlie added, "Nethercreatures are supposed to escape from the Nether and come to Earth, right? But the Dangeroo didn't do that. It came out of the Nether, grabbed Violet, and then went back in." He shrugged. "It doesn't make any sense. I mean, where was it taking her?"

"That's exactly what I asked while I was in its pouch," Violet said.

Everyone turned to her.

"And what did the critter say?" Rex prompted.

"Well, it was kind of hard to understand—its voice was pretty growly—but it sounded something like it was taking me to the Guardian."

Rex, Tabitha, and Pinch shared a troubled glance.

"You're sure?" Tabitha asked.

Violet shrugged. "Pretty sure."

What the heck's the Guardian? Charlie thought. *And why is everyone looking so serious all of a sudden?*

"Hooo-boy," Rex exclaimed. "Y'all thinkin' what I'm thinkin'?"

Tabitha nodded. "We'd better go see the Head-master."

She began to open a portal.

"That is, indeed, cause for great alarm," the Head-master of the Nightmare Academy said after Charlie finished telling her what had happened. She absently stroked a pet Snark that clung to a wooden railing on the first floor of her warm and pleasantly cluttered study.

"So, what do you think?" Rex asked. "You think the Named are behind this?"

Headmaster Brazenhope nodded. "Oh, most certainly. Slagguron and Tyrannus have been trying to escape from the Nether for centuries. If they're doing what I think they're doing, they may have finally found a way."

"Slagguron and Tyrannus?" Charlie asked. He'd heard those names once before. Six months earlier, he'd faced off against Barakkas and Verminion—two of the four Named Lords of the Nether—and barely escaped with his life and the lives of his friends and parents. Even though Barakkas and Verminion had made their way to Earth, he knew that the remaining two Named—Slagguron and Tyrannus—were still stranded in the Nether, where they lived in their dark and glorious palaces.

"What will they do if they get to Earth?" Violet asked.

"Summon the Fifth," Charlie replied quietly.

The very thought sent a chill through his heart. Each of the Named possessed an Artifact of the Nether. For Barakkas, it was a giant metal bracer around his wrist; for Verminion it was a thick choker around his neck. Charlie didn't know what type of artifacts the remaining two Named possessed, but he did know that if all four of them got together on Earth, they could use their artifacts together to summon a creature they called "The Fifth."

"What is it, exactly?" Violet asked.

"We don't yet know," the Headmaster replied. "But if the Named want to bring it here, it must be a monster of unimaginable evil."

"Then we'll monkey-stomp it!" Theodore blurted.

Everyone turned to him.

"Zipping the old lip, now," Theodore said, laughing uneasily. He pretended to zip his lips and throw away the key.

"The entire plan," the Headmaster continued, "hinges on Slagguron and Tyrannus being able to escape from the Nether to join Barakkas and Verminion here on Earth. Right now, the Guardian is the only thing preventing that from happening."

"What's the Guardian?" Charlie asked.

"A very unusual creature with a very *unique* ability: Any monsters that come near it are instantly crippled. It protects a weak spot between our world and the Nether called the Anomaly. Slagguron and Tyrannus are desperate to come through the Anomaly to Earth, but as long as the Guardian is there, they *can't*."

"What I don't get," Violet said, "is what all of this has to do with Dangeroos stealing kids."

The Headmaster turned to her. "That's quite simple. Just as the Guardian is poisonous to monsters, humans are poisonous to the Guardian. One touch from a human is enough to kill it."

"Which is why we think the Named plan to steal kids during their nightmares," Tabitha added, "and then bring them near the Guardian."

"Of course!" Theodore exclaimed. "Then the kids will run to the Guardian for protection. If they touch it, they'll kill it, and Slagguron and Tyrannus can escape to Earth through the Anomaly! That's brilliant!"

Violet stared at him, aghast.

"In a totally sick and evil way, I mean."

"Well, here's the million-dollar question," Rex said, scratching the stubble on his chin. "Are we too late? What I mean is, have ol' Slagguron and Tyrannus gotten to the Guardian already?"

"Let's find out." The Headmaster walked to the center of her study. Her white dress flowed behind her, highlighting her lovely dark skin, the color of burned caramel. She held out her right hand. Purple flames instantly crackled across her.

"What's she doing?" Theodore asked.

Charlie shrugged. "No idea."

Rex drew his gleaming short sword. "Y'all might want to step back—this could get ugly."

Charlie knew from experience that when Rex said something could get ugly, it could get *really* ugly. He, Theodore, and Violet stepped back.

"Be ready," the Headmaster said darkly. With startling ease, she opened a large portal. Through it, Charlie could see sharp, mustard-colored crystals glowing gloomily in the Nether.

"That's the 5th Ring," Theodore whispered. "Why did she open a portal to there?"

Before anyone could venture an answer, a Class-5 Silvertongue scuttled through and into the Headmaster's study. It looked like a giant scorpion, its poisonous stinger raised high above its head, ready to strike. Rex's short sword glowed brightly blue as he moved toward the monster to fend off an attack, but before he even got near it, the Silvertongue shrieked in agony and then dropped to the floor of the study, shuddering.

"What's happening?" Violet asked.

"That's what the Guardian's aura does to monsters of the Nether," Tabitha replied. "That's how we stay protected from them—no Nethercreatures can get to us here at the Academy as long as the Guardian is healthy."

That left one giant question: *How* did the Guardian's aura protect the Academy? The Academy wasn't in the Nether and certainly wasn't anywhere near the Guardian—or at least Charlie didn't *think* it was— so how did the Guardian's aura reach it?

As Charlie pondered that, Rex walked up to the writhing Silvertongue. Using all his weight, he shoved it back into the Nether through the Headmaster's portal. With a wave of her hand, she snapped it closed.

"The Academy's defenses are still strong," she said, "so we know that the Guardian is safe—but it won't remain that way for long. Eventually, the Named will succeed in exposing it to a human . . . unless we stop them."

But before Charlie could ask *how*, another portal snapped open in the room and a large man stepped through. He was as straight and tall as the two-handed sword sheathed at his side.

"Dad!" Theodore exclaimed.

The man turned and silently inspected him.

"Theodore," he said finally, without much emotion. "You've grown."

"Thanks!"

"Taller . . . but not wider. How do you expect to wield a weapon, skinny as you are?"

Theodore seemed to deflate. "But, Dad—you know I'm not a Banisher. I'm a Nethermancer, remember?"

"How could I forget?" He smiled grimly.

The way Theodore's father treated his son always turned Charlie's stomach. Sure, Theodore wasn't a Banisher like the rest of the Dagget family, but he was an awesomely good Nethermancer. Didn't that count for something?

"What brings you to us, William?" the Headmaster asked.

"*General* Dagget, if you don't mind."

"General!" Theodore blurted. "No way! Congrats, dad!"

"Thank you," William replied coolly.

"So how can we help you . . . , General?" the Headmaster asked.

"Director Drake demands your presence immediately."

"Excellent. There is much I need to discuss with him. There is terrible trouble in the Nether."

"Not just you—*all* of you." William glanced

around at the others in the room.

"Great," Rex grumbled. "Nothing I like more than getting marched over to the principal's office. He gonna paddle us? Make us stand in the corner with a dunce cap on our heads?"

"You better hope that's *all* he does," William replied. "I'm not sure I've ever seen him this furious."

Chapter Four

The Furious
Rememberer

D ay or night, the Nightmare Division was always the same. Windowless and sterile, it was an immensity of blinking, chirping electronics, and it always seemed to be filled with adult Banishers and Nethermancers racing to repair a disaster or escort a Nethercreature to one of the hundreds of containment rooms in the secure facility.

"Let me do the talking," the Headmaster said as she steered them expertly through a maze of hallways. "I think we all know how difficult and unpredictable the Director can be."

"You can say that again," Theodore moaned. "That guy's a nut!"

Suddenly, a Class-3 Acidspitter herded by four Banishers broke free from its muzzle and sprayed acid at them as they passed. Without even breaking stride, the Headmaster casually opened a portal between the group and the creature, allowing the burning fluid to spray harmlessly into the Nether. Within moments, the Banishers subdued the monster, and the Headmaster dismissed her portal.

Charlie marveled, as he had so many times before, at how powerful and fast she was.

"Here we are," the Headmaster said as they stopped at the sleek steel door marked OFFICE OF THE DIRECTOR—PRIVATE. "Remember, whatever happens, let me handle it."

The Director of the Nightmare Division was a tall man with steel gray hair and gray eyes to match. In fact, he was so gray that he almost seemed to disappear into the metal walls of his chambers. His manicured fingers tapped incessantly on his chrome desktop as he stared at Charlie down his long, crooked nose.

"Charlie Benjamin," he said slowly. Then: "I *remember*."

Charlie's blood froze.

"You remember?" he echoed uncertainly.

"Yes," the Director replied, savoring the word like a candy that delivers new flavors the harder you suck it. "I remember how you brought Barakkas into our world, in spite of my dire warnings. I remember how I sentenced you to be Reduced so that you could never again harm us. I remember how your friends and teachers came to your aid against my direct orders. In short, I remember . . . everything."

Charlie felt light-headed. He desperately wanted to sit down, put his head between his knees, close his eyes, and pretend this was all a bad dream—but he knew better.

Unfortunately, all the things the Director said were true: Charlie *had* allowed Barakkas to come to Earth and join Verminion. It had been accidental, of course. Charlie's untrained power was so strong that, under horrible stress, he had mistakenly opened a portal into the Inner Circle of the Nether, and Barakkas had rushed through.

As a result, the Director had called for Charlie to be "Reduced"—a quaint name for a barbaric surgical procedure that would have forever stripped Charlie of the ability to portal or banish. In fact, it had been done to Pinch as a child, leaving him bitter and powerless. The Headmaster, Rex, and Tabitha had flatly refused to allow that to happen to Charlie, which placed them all squarely in the Director's crosshairs.

"You're probably wondering how I remember?" the Director said, getting up from behind his desk and walking toward them. He ran his long fingers through his slicked-back gray hair, releasing the odor of the grooming product he'd used to style it—something almondy. "God knows you did everything on heaven and earth and *elsewhere* to make me forget."

And there it was, finally.

The Hags, Charlie thought, sick to his stomach. *He knows about the Hags of the Void.*

"You must have thought you were so clever," the Director said, his eyes drawn down to slits, "using the Queen of the Hags to take away my memories of your crimes. How brilliant you all must have thought you were. How remarkably devious."

"What's he talking about?" Theodore whispered.

"I have no idea," Violet said with a shrug.

But I sure do, Charlie thought grimly.

He hadn't been there when the Headmaster, Rex, and Tabitha kidnapped the Director and brought him to the Queen of the Hags, but he had seen what the foul beast could do. She flew toward you on her powerful leather wings, enfolded you in them, and then, leaning back her green scaly head, she snaked a shockingly long tongue through her forest of teeth and plunged it into your ear, where she sucked deeply of—

Your memories.

She ate them like chocolate candies, and when she was done, you lost them forever.

Except not this time.

The Hag Queen had taken from the Director all the memories of Charlie and his friends . . . but somehow he had gotten them back.

"How?" Charlie asked. "How did you remember?"

"Look around you." Director Drake gestured at the remarkable electronics of the Nightmare Division. "Everything that happens here is recorded and catalogued. It was only a matter of time before the members of my council showed me those recordings . . . reminded me what you had done to me, what *all* of you had done to me." He leaned in so close that Charlie could see the coffee stains on his teeth. "Or did you think I would never find out?"

"Of course we expected you to find out," the Headmaster replied, startling Charlie. He had forgotten she was even in the room.

"And what did you plan to do then?"

"Why, take you back to the Hag, of course. Get your memory wiped, like we always do."

"Like you always . . ." Director Drake's face suddenly went the color of ash. With his gray hair and gray eyes, he looked like the tin man from some evil, alternate version of *The Wizard of Oz*. "You don't actually mean you—"

"Oh, Reginald," the Headmaster interrupted. "You

can't possibly think this is the first time you've remembered, do you? Why in the world would the council have waited six months to show you the recordings of our conflicts? They did it right away, of course, and, right away, we brought you back to the Hag to have your memory wiped again."

"What?" the Director gasped, and Charlie almost, *almost*, felt a little sorry for him. "How many times have you let that . . . creature . . . have her way with me?"

The Headmaster glanced off in thought. "I'm not sure. It's so hard to keep track . . ."

"Seven," Rex drawled. "'Least, that's how many times I remember."

"Seven," the Headmaster agreed with a firm nod. "That sounds right."

"You've done this to me *seven* times?"

"Yes, and it is just as distasteful for us as I'm sure it is for you. Unfortunately, your rage toward Charlie Benjamin has made it necessary. Clearly, this is an issue we will have to resolve, but now is not the time—we have far more pressing matters to attend to. There is something potentially catastrophic happening in the Nether. The Guardian—"

"I don't care about the Guardian!" Director Drake snapped. "I care about seeing all of you suffer the punishment you most certainly deserve!"

And, without another word, he reached under his desk and pressed a button. Red lights started flashing throughout the Nightmare Division as sirens wailed.

"He hit the alarm!" Violet yelled. "We're gonna get caught!"

"Oh, I hope so," Director Drake replied. "But don't worry, little girl—I'll do you the favor of sending you to the Reduction room *last.*"

"Lemme at him!" Theodore yelled, rushing toward the man, but Charlie held him back.

"Settle down, sprout," Rex said, unlooping his lasso from his belt. "Nothing's gonna happen to us, trust me." He turned to Tabitha. "Make a portal, would ya, darlin'?"

"Where to?"

"Why, the Hags, of course."

Director Drake stumbled backward, steadying himself on the edge of his desk. "No . . . this is treason."

"He says that every time, don't he?" Rex said with a chuckle. Then, with one quick snap of his wrist, the lasso sailed across the Director's study and pulled tight around the man's chest, pinning his arms to his sides.

"Let's go, pardner. You got a date with a beautiful lady."

The Queen of the Hags was gnawing off her toenails with her teeth when the group portaled into the grand ballroom of her crumbling manor in the Nether. She glanced up at them from her stained throne but kept chewing away at a particularly thick, stubborn nail as if the arrival of the humans was not much of a surprise. Several Hags in dirty ball gowns stood in attendance, brushing her matted hair with fine, silver combs.

"Wow," Theodore said, looking around in dismay. "This place is gross!"

"No kidding," Violet agreed.

"We're back," Rex said, yanking the Director forward with his lasso.

The Hag Queen finally bit off the particularly troublesome toenail and spat it across the ballroom with surprising force. The hard, yellow crescent stuck into the finely carved wooden mantel above the giant fireplace like a dart.

"Indeed you are," she said, licking her black lips. "And I see you've brought the Director again."

"We have," the Headmaster said, walking toward the monstrous parody of a woman. "I hope you're hungry."

"Always," the Hag Queen replied, then yelped in pain. "You hit a tangle!" She turned to the Hag at her left, and, with one swipe of her taloned claw, sliced the creature's head cleanly from its body. Black ichor fountained up as the dead Hag collapsed to the floor, dropping its silver comb with a clatter.

"Really," the Hag Queen said with a disgusted sigh as she rose into the air on her leathery wings, stirring up so much dust that the ballroom looked like a Texas prairie. "A good lady-in-hating is impossible to find. You beg them to be gentle, but they always disappoint. I'm a delicate flower, you know."

"And a beautiful one," Rex chimed in, giving her his best smile.

"Oh, *you*," the beast replied with a girlish giggle. The sound made Charlie's stomach heave. "Always a charmer."

"I just call 'em as I see 'em, Miss."

"Miss!" the Hag Queen echoed with a howl. "I love that. Are you sure you won't let me have another taste of those delicious memories you keep locked away inside that handsome skull? A sweet little bonbon from your past?" She swooped toward him and brushed his ear with her black lips. "Your first kiss, perhaps?" she cooed sickeningly.

"I'm afraid we have more pressing business," the Headmaster said.

"Ugh, you don't really want me to drain the memory of that crusty old relic again, do you?" The

Hag Queen nodded to the Director. "I won't do it, you know. His hatred of the boy is stale. It's a memory of a memory of a memory. He doesn't truly hate the boy anymore, anyway—he only knows that he should."

Charlie turned to the Director. "Is that true?"

"Of course not!" the Director snapped. Then he seemed to realize that he was arguing in favor of having his memory drained by a monster. "I mean . . . hasn't this all gone too far? Aren't there alternatives?"

"Oh, I agree completely," the Headmaster replied. "I would love to put an end to this madness. As I said, we have serious matters to attend to, life-or-death concerns. Perhaps it's time for a truce."

"A truce," the Director echoed. "Yes. Perhaps that is prudent. In the best interest of everyone."

But before he could speak another word, the ground beneath them began to shake violently. At first Charlie thought it was an earthquake, but he could tell by the panic that flooded the Hag Queen's eyes that it was something far worse.

"No," she said, rising higher into the air on her strong wings. "He's near."

"He?" Charlie asked.

The stained-glass windows in the ballroom shook crazily as the rumbling intensified and a ripple like a giant wave passed under the manor, buckling the ancient stone floor.

Something huge had moved through the ground beneath their feet.

Something monstrous.

Everyone was thrown to the floor as the chandeliers came loose from their ceiling anchors and plummeted down like glass bombs.

"Cover your eyes!" Rex yelled.

Charlie and his friends did—just in time to avoid being blinded by the fragments. Soon, the violent rumbling lessened and everyone was able to stand. The ground beneath their feet spasmed once . . . twice . . . then grew still.

"What was that?" Violet asked after a moment, breaking the silence.

"That," the Hag Queen replied as she hovered high in the air, "was Slagguron."

"The Third Named," the Headmaster said softly, eyeing the massive damage the monster had inflicted just by passing *near* them. It was one of the few times Charlie had seen her look impressed.

"He travels underground?" Tabitha asked.

"Didn't you know?" The Hag Queen seemed genuinely surprised.

"We've never seen him," Director Drake said, finally shrugging Rex's lasso from around his chest.

"We've heard rumors, of course, and one of them was that he was like a giant worm that traveled through the Nethercrust, but they were never confirmed."

"Consider them confirmed." The Hag Queen settled back down on the buckled ground. "He's been very active lately, tunneling through much of the Nether. Never before has he strayed from his palace in the Inner Circle." She smiled secretively. "But, of course, there is much that is strange in the Nether, of late."

Just then, a shriek ripped through the air with such intensity that the stained-glass windows exploded from the vibration. A sound like a jet engine roared closer.

"Look!" Theodore yelled and pointed. "That thing's ridiculous!"

Through the broken window, Charlie could see a golden streak in the sky, flapping magnificently against the red, fiery tornado of the Inner Circle far in the distance.

"Tyrannus," the Headmaster whispered. "The Fourth Named."

The streak moved through the alien air of the Nether with astonishing speed, and Charlie could make out a vague, batlike presence—it flew so fast that he couldn't see much more than a blur. Then there was that shriek again, so deafening that Charlie felt his bones vibrate. The flying, golden monstrosity roared overhead, filling the world with thunder and shattering the already broken pieces of glass into a fine powder.

"What the heck's going on around here?" Rex asked, astonished. "First Slagguron, then Tyrannus. The Named have never acted like this!"

A crazy cackle ripped through the air as Tyrannus looped back around and soared high above the crumbling manor of the Hags.

"VICTORY!" he screeched in his insanely shrill voice. "Monsters of the Nether, REJOICE! We have WON! The Guardian is DONE and now we will have our FUN!"

"No," Tabitha gasped.

"This," the Headmaster said, turning to Director Drake, "is what I was afraid of. I must go to the Guardian immediately."

"I'll go with you," Tabitha said.

"May as well count me in, too," Rex added. "You're gonna have to take me anyway. The princess here"—he nodded to Tabitha—"can't stand to be away from yours truly for too long."

"Oh, please."

The Headmaster shook her head. "I'm sorry. I appreciate your offer, both of you, but I must go alone. You've not been around the Guardian before, but I've spent many long days with that gentle creature. I know its unique problems . . . and its odd desires . . . and I know how to resist them."

"You're being foolish, Brazenhope," Director Drake snorted. "If the Guardian is weakened or dying, who knows how many Nethercreatures may be closing in on it? If there's to be a fight, our strength lies in our numbers."

"This is not a fight of force, Reginald," the Headmaster replied, "but of subtlety. Besides, you will all be engaged in a much greater task. The time has come, I'm afraid, to put into effect a plan I had dearly hoped to avoid."

She glanced at each of them in turn, her eyes gravely serious.

"You must begin the Division Invasion."

· CHAPTER FIVE ·
THE DIVISION INVASION

The High Council Chamber of the Nightmare Division was packed. Adult Banishers and Nethermancers stirred restlessly in their seats, then quieted as the Director took his place at the dais.

"I have just left an engagement with the Headmaster," he said, after clearing his throat. "And we have come to an agreement. There is now a truce in place regarding the matter of Charlie Benjamin."

Charlie shifted uncomfortably in his chair as all the adults strained to see him.

"What are you lookin' at?" Theodore said, staring them down. "This isn't the circus."

The adults glanced away.

"Because of alarming new developments, everyone associated with Charlie Benjamin's past misconduct is hereby pardoned, which clears the way for us to confront the greatest threat we have ever faced."

He began to pace.

"Ladies and gentlemen, something extraordinary is happening in the Nether, and we must act immediately or find ourselves in a war with unimaginable consequences. We have reason to believe that the Guardian has been weakened and that Slagguron and Tyrannus may soon escape to join Barakkas and Verminion here on Earth. I don't need to remind you that, if they succeed, the four Named will be able to use their artifacts in concert to summon the Fifth. If that happens, the Nethercreatures will begin a full-scale assault on our world—unless we stop them. Unfortunately, we have no choice but to implement a plan we had hoped to avoid: the Division Invasion."

He turned to William, who stood behind him on the dais. "General Dagget? Please fill us in."

Rex groaned. "Oh, come on. He put this idiot in charge?" And that's when he noticed Theodore beside him. "Sorry, kid," Rex continued, a little sheepishly. "I know he's your dad and all, but it's no secret that William and I haven't always seen eye to eye."

"It's okay," Theodore replied. "Neither have we."

William stepped up to the front of the dais and coolly surveyed the assembled Banishers and Nethermancers in front of him.

"If all four Named escape to Earth, there is only one way to prevent them from using their artifacts together to summon the Fifth."

He gazed at them stonily.

"One of the Named must die."

The room was as still and quiet as a tomb. Even Charlie wasn't quite sure he'd heard right.

"How is that even possible?" someone finally shouted.

"We don't stand a chance against a Named!" another said.

And then the floodgates opened. All the Banishers and Nethermancers began talking rapidly, loudly debating what most of them seemed to consider a clearly suicidal plan.

As they argued, a long, loud whistle pierced the clamor, and one by one the voices grew silent. To Charlie's astonishment, he realized that the whistle had come from Rex.

"I know what y'all are thinkin'," the cowboy said, standing. "Killing a Named is like staring down the barrel of a gun and hopin' to catch the bullet with your teeth. It's a tall gulp of water—no question about it—but we gotta drink it eventually, and I don't see our chances getting any better by puttin' it off. Heck, thanks to Charlie Benjamin here"—he tilted his hat in

Charlie's direction, and Charlie flushed with embarrassment—"Barakkas and Verminion were wounded pretty bad a while back."

Charlie's mind flashed to the last time he'd seen the two Named. As a result of his trickery, the giant beasts fought furiously with each other in their lair underneath Krakatoa. They tore each other apart so completely that Charlie wasn't even sure they could have survived.

"Who knows?" Rex continued. "Maybe one of those bad boys is already dead and our job's done for us. Point is, we gotta make sure, and we gotta do it now while we still got the upper hand." He turned to William. "You know I can't stand you, Big Bill—but on this one, I'm with you."

"Thank you, Banisher Henderson," the General replied. "Ladies and gentlemen, prepare for combat."

Just over an hour later, forty Banishers and Nethermancers were assembled on the barren plains of the 1st Ring of the Nether. Never before had there been such a collection of skill and ability focused on a single purpose. As William walked among them, surveying their preparations, he noticed Charlie, Violet, and Theodore.

"What are the children doing here? This is no place for them."

"I asked Charlie to join us," Rex said, walking up. "He's portaled to the lair of the Named more than anyone else here, which means he's got the best chance of portaling us back there cleanly."

"Fine. But that doesn't explain why the other two are here," He nodded to Theodore and Violet. "The boy and the girl."

The boy, Charlie thought wryly. *Don't you mean "my son"?*

"Someone's got to protect Charlie!" Theodore exclaimed. "And that someone is me! If Charlie goes, so do I—that's TNN, Totally non-negotiable!"

"Really?" William allowed a hint of a smile to escape. "But you're just a Nethermancer. Wouldn't he be better off under the protection of a Banisher?"

"That's why I'm here," Violet said, stepping forward. "Theodore and I will keep Charlie safe while the rest of you fight."

"I see. The Three Musketeers, is it?"

Charlie, Violet, and Theodore nodded.

"So be it." William turned to Rex. "You've had some experience with Barakkas and Verminion before. What do you expect we'll find when Charlie opens the portal?"

"Well, I can't tell you which Named is gonna be closest, but if we're facing off against Verminion, I'd say go for the neck—you'll never get through his shell. If we're looking at Barakkas, aim for the heart and, for the love of God, watch those horns of his unless you feel like bein' a shish kebab."

There was a smattering of grim laughter.

"Whoever we tackle," Rex continued, "we gotta do it hard and we gotta do it fast before the whole dang army of the Nether comes down on top of us."

"Thank you," William said. "I'll take over now, if you don't mind." He turned from Rex and addressed the crowd. "Nethermancers, I will want a portal barricade around the Banishers to catch the reinforcements as new monsters swarm in from the tunnels. And Nethermancer Greenstreet—"

William glanced over at Tabitha. She seemed surprised to have been singled out.

"Yes?"

"If it looks like a wipe, you're in charge of the wetwash."

"Will do."

Portal barricade? Wetwash? Charlie had no idea what William was talking about. He felt desperately out of his league.

"All right then," William said. "Banishers, check your gear."

There was a tremendous sound of clanging steel as

the many Banishers inspected their weaponry. Shiny axes, gleaming maces, and a dozen varieties of swords glowed fiery blue in the vast wasteland of the Nether.

"Everyone good?"

There were nods of assent.

"Then let's do this. Charlie?"

"Yes, sir," Charlie replied.

"Open the portal."

Charlie nodded. He was so nervous that his mouth had gone as dry as sandpaper.

"Hey, kid," Rex whispered, "if you get in trouble, you just give a shout and I'll come runnin', got me?"

"Will do," Charlie said. He closed his eyes and opened a portal to Verminion's lair underneath Krakatoa.

The elite Banishers and Nethermancers of the Nightmare Division rushed through the portal into the gargantuan cavern with a furious battle cry. Heat washed over Charlie and his friends like a tidal wave, emanating from the many glowing pools of bubbling lava that cast hazy, uncertain light across the twisted rock formations that had formed in the vast emptiness over centuries.

Charlie's heart thudded crazily in his chest as they all raced through the lair, expecting to be attacked by hundreds of monsters at any second. Charlie looked around frantically for signs of Verminion . . . or Barakkas . . . or anything.

But the cavern was empty.

The two Named, along with their army, were gone.

"You're kidding me," Rex said, glancing around at the vacant chamber that surrounded them.

"They *were* here," Charlie said, staring in amazement. "I opened a portal to the right place, honest."

"We know, kid," Rex replied. "But it looks like they've moved on. They're already one step ahead of us."

Just then, a clatter of falling stone came from behind them. They spun to see a Class-4 Netherstalker scuttling into the cavern on its eight spider legs, seemingly unaware of the massive intrusion.

"Get it!" William yelled, and the horde of Banishers raced toward the lone creature.

It tried to escape, but the squad quickly subdued it. William drew his two-handed sword and held the brightly burning blade against the writhing creature's neck. It sizzled.

"Where have they gone?" he demanded.

The Netherstalker hissed at him, and William leaned on the blade hard enough to cut through its carapace and draw a line of flowing black ichor. "You tell me, monster, or you'll experience pain you can't imagine."

"Wait!" Charlie yelled. The adults turned to him. "Don't hurt it. There's a better way."

Charlie led Professor Xixclix into the volcanic lair through a new portal.

"Greetings," the friendly Netherstalker said to the raid party, cleaning a spiderlike foreleg with his bristly tongue. "Charlie tells me you've found another of my kind."

"He's right over there," Charlie said, pointing to the captured Netherstalker. "Can you talk to him? We need to find out where Verminion and Barakkas went."

"Shouldn't be too difficult," Xix replied. "He's only a Class 4. Having just acquired Class-5 status myself, I shouldn't have much trouble getting him to crack."

Charlie was amused to discover a hint of pride in the beast's voice.

Xix scuttled over to the kidnapped Netherstalker and began to speak to him in their own tongue: hisses and clicks and the occasional spitting sound. It was the first time Charlie had seen Xix among his own kind. He had grown so used to seeing the creature in his normal role as the Academy's Beastmaster that he'd almost forgotten he wasn't human—although it was hard to look at the large, spiderlike beast with the barbed hairs on his spindly legs and the streaked violet pattern on his shiny black back and think he was anything *other* than a monster.

"So . . . you been okay?" William asked Theodore as the creatures conversed. Charlie was surprised by the question—nothing about William's previous attitude suggested he was even remotely interested in his son.

"Great!" Theodore answered, clearly as shocked by the question as Charlie. "I really love the Academy!"

"He's one of the best Nethermancers there," Violet added.

"Definitely," Charlie said.

William glanced at the three of them, then turned to Theodore. "It was a good thing you did, insisting on coming here to help your friend. I like that."

Theodore looked utterly astonished. "Well . . . thanks!" He broke out in a wide, crooked grin.

Just then, Xix stepped nimbly over to them, having finished talking to the captured creature.

"Well?" William asked.

"He doesn't know much," Xix replied. "But he does know that they've relocated the lair to the 'Frozen Wastes,' wherever that is. His job was to stay behind and flood the old lair with lava to erase all evidence of their ever having been here."

"Sounds like he drew the short straw," Rex said.

"So what do they want?" Charlie asked. "Barakkas and Verminion, I mean? What are they trying to do?"

But before Xix could ask the captured creature, it answered on its own—

"Kill . . . everyone . . ."

The assembled Banishers and Nethermancers glanced uneasily at one another.

"We gotta find 'em," Rex said. "Wherever they are, we gotta hunt down those Named and kill one of 'em, and we can't stop until we do."

Charlie's stomach felt sour. Killing one of the Named was a nearly impossible task to begin with, but now they didn't even know where Barakkas and Verminion *were*. Already they had suffered a serious defeat—and they hadn't even begun to fight. In time, it was possible they could discover the location of the new lair, but was there enough time?

It's all up to the Headmaster now, Charlie thought.

He hoped she'd found the Guardian alive.

He hoped she'd be able to keep it that way.

He hoped it wasn't too late.

PART
· II ·
The Guardian

· CHAPTER SIX ·
INTO THE DEPTHS

The Nightmare Academy was always a welcome sight—those massive wrecked ships sitting on the branches of the world's most gigantic banyan tree never failed to leave Charlie awestruck—but this time he was so upset that he barely gave it a glance.

"What's wrong, Charlie?" Violet asked as she finished the last of the mango she was having for lunch. "We haven't even been back a whole day, and you look like an Ectobog swallowed your mother."

"What's wrong?" he snapped. "What's *not* wrong! Rex and Tabitha are trying to find Verminion's new lair on Earth; the Headmaster is in the Nether, trying to help the Guardian . . ."

"So?"

"So we're stuck here doing nothing!"

"Aha!" Violet exclaimed. "You're just angry that we're out of the action. Relax. Our part in this is done. We're just Noobs."

"Addys," Theodore quickly corrected her. "I don't care what Pinch said. We still have to get a ruling from the Headmaster on that when she gets back."

"Well, my point is that serious stuff is going on and it's no longer our responsibility."

"You're right." Charlie sighed. "But that doesn't mean we can't help in some way."

Frustrated, he leaned against the railing of the pirate ship and stared out at the ocean beyond.

"Hey, guys."

Charlie turned to see Brooke, with her blond hair and blue eyes, rise up through a veil of leaves like some kind of angel ascending. She stepped off the elevator-like dinghy that carried her there and walked toward them with a flawless smile.

"Hey, Brooke!" Charlie and Theodore chirped at the same time.

Violet rolled her eyes. Yes, Brooke was older and taller and beautiful, but really!

"So what's going on?" Brooke asked.

"Major, major stuff," Theodore replied, "but Charlie's mad because he's not part of it."

Charlie glared at him.

"I mean, we're *all* mad about that," Theodore quickly added. "Not just Charlie—I didn't mean to single him out like he's some kind of pouty preschooler or something."

"That's exactly what he is," a familiar voice said.

Charlie glanced over to see Geoff—Brooke's big, blond boyfriend—walking up behind her with a snide look. It pained Charlie that the boy only seemed to grow more handsome with age: He was sixteen but looked twenty.

"After all," Geoff continued, "you're all still just Noobs. Everyone knows you failed your final."

"We did not fail it!" Theodore shot back. "The Headmaster hasn't given us a ruling, so the jury's still out."

"That's not the only thing that's out. *You're* out—of your mind!" Geoff snorted with laughter and looked to Brooke for approval.

"Why don't you go and find something to do that doesn't involve me?" she replied coolly.

Charlie wanted to cheer but tactfully looked away. Theodore, however, went ahead and cheered.

"Shut it!" Geoff roared, raising his fist.

Theodore raised his fist back at the much larger boy. Then, using his thumb and forefinger like a puppet mouth, he said "I love you!" in a squeaky falsetto and kissed Geoff's fist with his own.

Geoff stared at him, dumbfounded, then turned to Brooke. "These are the people you wanna hang with?"

"That's right."

"Well, if you get tired of playing kindergarten, you come see me." He stomped across the deck to a waiting dinghy and dropped quickly out of sight.

"Boys . . . ," Brooke said to Violet with a dramatic sigh as if they were both battle-hardened veterans of the dating game. "They follow you around like gum on your shoe and get so upset when you scrape them off."

"I don't chew gum," Violet replied curtly.

"Meow!" Theodore exclaimed. "Kitty likes to scratch! *Rawwwr!*" He raked the air in front of Violet with a pretend claw.

"I think I'm done here," Violet huffed, turning to go.

"Wait!" Brooke called after her.

Charlie knew that Violet had never much liked Brooke—couldn't stand her, actually—because of the older girl's supposed snottiness. But Charlie also knew from his time fighting beside Brooke in Verminion's lair that her superior attitude was really hiding a terrible insecurity.

"You can't leave yet," Brooke continued. "I have a message for you from the Headmaster. For all of you, actually."

"When did you see the Headmaster?" Violet asked,

turning back, suddenly interested.

"Yesterday. She talked to me just before she headed into the Nether."

Must have been right after she left us with the Hag Queen, Charlie realized. "What did she say?"

"She said that if she didn't return by noon today, the four of us should go and meet her in the Nether."

"But she was going to the Guardian," Charlie exclaimed. "I don't have a clue where in the Nether it is!"

Brooke shrugged. "Doesn't matter, really. You can't portal directly to the Guardian anyway. You can only portal *near* it into an area that's superdangerous. The Headmaster can handle herself there, but it's too tough for us. That's why we have to use the Guardian boat."

The three friends exchanged glances.

"What's the Guardian boat?" Charlie asked.

The Guardian boat was hidden under the leaves of a banana tree in a rocky cove farther south on the island than Charlie and his friends had ever ventured.

"Look at this thing!" Theodore exclaimed as they climbed inside the small craft. About the size of a speedboat, it had six seats, each with a steel safety restraint. The bar came down over the shoulders and across the chest. Theodore enthusiastically latched himself in. "Check it out! It's like the kind of thing you see on one of those upside-down rollercoasters."

"That's disturbing," Violet remarked. "Why would it need that?"

While Theodore messed around with the restraint, Charlie inspected the captain's chair. There were remarkably few controls on the dashboard in front of it: an ignition switch, a throttle for controlling the boat's speed, a steering wheel, a simple compass for telling direction, and a red button with the words WARNING: USE ONLY DURING FREEFALL etched below it.

"Freefall?" Charlie said. "What's that for?"

Brooke shrugged. "Don't know. All I know is you're supposed to head into the ocean and somehow the boat gets you there."

"Somehow the boat *gets you there*?" Violet asked dubiously. "You mean you just—poof!—magically end up near the Guardian?"

"Well, that's what the Headmaster said," Brooke replied, a little defensively. "Obviously, I've never done it."

"Great," Violet moaned. "That's comforting. We have no idea how this thing is even supposed to work!"

"Aside from that red button and the weird seat-belts," Charlie said, "it basically looks pretty much like a regular boat. We just need someone to steer it out of the cove and not smash us up on the rocks."

"I'll do it," Theodore said. "I'm great at steering boats!"

"Really?" Charlie asked. "Have you ever steered one before?"

"No."

"Then how do you know you're great at it?"

"Have you even met me?" Theodore replied. "This is the kind of thing I'm just naturally good at—duh." He unlatched the over-the-shoulder harness and stood up, but Violet pushed him back down.

"I'll pilot it," she said, sitting in the captain's chair. "My family used to have a boat. Buckle up."

Charlie, Brooke, and Theodore did as they were told. Violet turned on the ignition, moved the throttle forward, and gently guided the small craft through the rocks and out of the cove.

"Hey, you're pretty good at this," Charlie said, admiring her skill.

"A girl's gotta be prepared."

The day was warm, the air was clear, and in spite of the danger and uncertainty of their mission, Charlie felt his spirits rise as they left the island behind them and sailed out into the welcoming arms of the open ocean.

The catastrophe started out small.

Twenty miles offshore, their compass needle, which had been pointing them steadily, reliably north, suddenly spun to the south, then east, then back south again.

"Weird," Violet said, watching it as it jittered uncertainly.

"Something wrong?" Charlie asked.

"Not sure. The compass just went funky. Look, there it goes again!"

The needle spun frantically to the left and then to the right.

"Don't worry about it," Theodore said. "Compass malfunctions like that are totally normal. Could be the gravitational pull of the moon, or maybe we're drifting over a large chunk of magnetized ore."

"What are you talking about?" Charlie replied. "Do you even have any idea what you're saying?" He pointed to the instrument panel. "Look at the thing—that's definitely not normal!"

The compass continued to spin crazily as the ocean grew choppy. Above them, the frothy, white clouds started to darken.

"Maybe we should turn around," Brooke suggested

uneasily. "Looks like a storm's coming."

"I would," Violet said, "but with the compass acting so funny, I'm not sure I could find our way back."

"Of course you can!" Theodore said. "Just use the sun."

"The sun?"

"You know, for navigation."

Violet gritted her teeth. "Okay, how?"

"How should I know? You're the captain. Duh."

It's a good thing she's restrained by that metal harness, Charlie thought, seeing the look of death in Violet's eyes.

"Just turn us around," he said calmly. "At least then we'll be heading away from the rough water."

The water was, in fact, starting to get rough. A heavy wind had kicked up, stinging their faces with salt spray. Charlie was shocked by how quickly the weather had turned against them.

"You may be right," Violet said a little nervously, glancing around as increasingly big waves pounded their small boat, causing it to soar and fall like a child's toy. She turned the wheel.

Nothing happened.

The boat continued to head in the same direction, seemingly drawn now by some strong, unseen force.

Huge ocean waves sloshed over the side, threatening to swamp them.

"What's wrong?" Charlie shouted over the rising howl of the wind.

"I don't know!" Violet yelled back. "It's like I'm not steering it anymore! Something's pulling us!"

"That's probably either the north or south pole," Theodore reasoned, "depending on what side of the globe we're on, of course."

"What?" Charlie yelled. "The Nightmare Academy is nowhere *near* the poles—it's someplace tropical, obviously!"

"You don't know where the Academy *is*?" Brooke asked incredulously as another massive wave washed over them.

"Well, no!" Charlie shouted back, wiping the stinging ocean water from his eyes. "No one's ever told us!"

"I guess that's not so strange," Brooke reasoned. "They don't really teach you that stuff until you're an Addy."

"So where are we?" Theodore screamed.

Rain began to lash them in thick sheets. Lightning cracked across the dark sky.

"The Bermuda Triangle," Brooke shouted as the boat began to spin wildly with the current. "The

Nightmare Academy is in the Bermuda Triangle!"

They stared at her, speechless.

"The Bermuda Freaking Triangle?" Theodore yelled. "Are you kidding me? We're in a death trap! Do you know how many planes and ships have been lost here?"

"Not really," Brooke shouted.

"Tons! This is unbelievable! We're gonna die!"

"Stop that!" Violet shouted. "We're not gonna die!"

"Actually," Charlie said, looking over the side, "I think we just might."

The ocean began to spin in a giant whirlpool, and their small craft raced crazily around its edges. Far below, deep beneath the churning water, they could see a gigantic glowing red disc.

It was an alien, incredible sight.

"What *is* that thing?" Brooke yelled, astonished.

"I have no idea!" Charlie shouted.

They shot down the center of the whirlpool until their tiny speedboat was plunged underwater, spiraling out of control, drawn by the strange red disc. As they neared it, Charlie began to realize how truly massive it was—at least a mile from side to side. It grew in his vision until it filled the world. He strained against his shoulder restraint, trying desperately to free himself, but the metal harness was now tightly locked. There was no way to escape from the small boat that was violently hurtling them through the cold, breathless depths, toward the swirling, mysterious object at the bottom of the sea.

· CHAPTER SEVEN ·
THE BT GRAVEYARD

Charlie couldn't breathe.

He didn't know how long he'd been under-water—maybe minutes, maybe only sec-onds—but he *did* know that if he didn't get oxygen soon, he was going to die. His lungs burned and a cold blackness began to close over his vision like a coffin lid. He could see his friends around him, drowning, unable to escape the sinking boat. His eyes locked onto Violet's. He saw panic in them . . . and also a dim acceptance.

His heart sank.

Once again, he had led them down a dark and lonely path that seemed to end in certain death. They were now so close to the giant, swirling disc beneath them that Charlie could reach out and touch it—which he tried to do.

But there was nothing to touch.

His hand passed through it, followed by the rest of the boat. And then they were falling, end over end, through the air—but it was air! Charlie gasped, breathing in deeply as the blessed oxygen put out the fire in his lungs. Even though they were tumbling wildly, the over-the-shoulder restraints kept them firmly secured in their seats. Charlie could see snapshot glimpses of things around him—the yellow of crystals, a pillar of red fire—

We're in the Nether, he suddenly realized. *We're free-falling through the Nether.*

Freefall.

Where had he seen that word before?

"Push the button!" he screamed at Violet. "The big red button on the dash—punch it!"

Violet, groggy and disoriented, saw the red button with the words WARNING: USE ONLY DURING FREEFALL. Focusing all her energy, she reached forward and pressed it.

There was an intense hissing sound, like air rushing from a tire. Transparent balloons burst out of the sides of the speedboat and inflated instantly. They covered the small craft in a kind of cocoon, slowing its descent. Through them, Charlie could see the blurry image of what looked like sailing ships—hundreds and hundreds of them—on the ground far below.

The Guardian boat plummeted down before finally slamming into the deck of an old freighter. It bounced up like a rubber ball, spinning as it did, and Charlie caught a dizzying glimpse of the enormous red disc through which they had fallen. It was now above them, glimmering in the distance.

And then they were falling again, tumbling wildly.

After a couple more bounces, their crazy speedboat came to a stop. The protective balloons deflated, and the over-the-shoulder restraints unlocked with a satisfying *clonk*.

They had arrived.

"Well . . . that was interesting," Theodore said, raising his restraint.

"Everyone okay?" Charlie asked as he unlatched himself.

"I'm not sure," Brooke replied, breathing frantically. "I think so. Do I look okay?"

"Heck, yeah!" Theodore said. "You look great."

"I'm okay, too, Theodore," Violet said wryly. "Just in case you were wondering."

"Oh, definitely. I was gonna check on you next. Totally."

"Uh-huh."

They all stepped out of the boat and looked

around. They were in the middle of a giant graveyard of wrecked ships, piled high like automobiles in a junk-yard. The ones on the bottom were old and weathered, getting newer the higher up the pile you looked. Above it all, the giant red disc—which Charlie now realized was some kind of portal—loomed like a dying sun.

"We call it 'the Anomaly,'" a voice behind them said.

They turned to see the Headmaster walking toward them, weaving her way deftly through the remains of the hulking, crippled ships.

"Headmaster!" Charlie exclaimed. "We got your message!"

"Yes, yes, I see that you did." Her eyes glinted in amusement. "You're standing in what's known as the BT Graveyard. Very few humans have ever laid eyes on it."

"BT Graveyard," Charlie repeated. "That stands for Bermuda Triangle Graveyard, right?"

The Headmaster nodded. "As you might have guessed, the Anomaly draws ships toward it from the Earth above and deposits them here."

"The Anomaly . . . this is what the Guardian pro-tects, isn't it?"

"Indeed. We're not sure what it is, exactly—some type of tear in the fabric of the Nether, perhaps."

If it's a tear, it sure is a big one, Charlie thought.

It was enormous—a hundred times larger than even the biggest portal he could open. It burned with a red fire instead of the usual purple. It seemed to remain always open and it actually attracted things to it, like a magnet, allowing everything but seawater to pass.

Not a drop comes through, he thought with amazement as he stared up at it. Just then, he noticed a large shadow approaching from the Earth side.

"What's that?" he asked.

"Something big," the Headmaster replied.

The thing that cast the shadow drew closer and closer until it fell through the Anomaly and into the Nether.

It can't be . . . , Charlie thought. *It's a humpback whale!*

The great creature plummeted down, writhing and twisting desperately through the air until it finally crashed into the ruins of an old plane in a tremendous explosion of steel and blubber.

"That poor thing!" Brooke said, clutching her chest.

"It's unfortunate, but it happens," the Headmaster replied. "Most sea creatures sense the Anomaly and avoid it, but occasionally one will get trapped. I would have opened a portal beneath it and allowed it to fall back into Earth's ocean, but you can't portal anywhere near the Anomaly—hence the need for the Guardian boat." She gestured toward their odd little craft. "It's an unconventional way to get here, to be sure, but it's also, amazingly, the safest. Without it, you'd have to portal into the 5th Ring and fight your way here through Class-5 monsters, as I did earlier. Not pleasant."

"Definitely not," Violet agreed.

"So the Anomaly is why the Bermuda Triangle gets such a bad rap?" Theodore said. "Why radar goes funky here, why so many people get lost and disappear. The mystery is solved!"

"Indeed it is, Mr. Dagget. The Anomaly allows things to cross from Earth into the Nether."

"Yeah," Charlie said. "And I'm guessing it also does the reverse: allow things to cross from the Nether into Earth. Things like monsters. Things like the Named."

The Headmaster nodded. "That's correct, Mr. Benjamin. It would . . . if it weren't protected by the Guardian."

"Where is it? The Guardian, I mean."

"Come," the Headmaster replied. "I'll show you."

The Guardian wasn't at all what Charlie expected.

Weak and fragile, it was the size of a child, with wide, watery eyes and translucent orange skin that revealed pulsing blue veins beneath. Its mouth was small, like a baby's, full of tiny, white teeth that shined like little pearls. It crossed its long, spindly arms over its thin chest and shivered, wheezing asthmatically.

"Hold me," it said in a whispery voice. "I'm cold."

The Guardian lived in the captain's quarters of a ruined warship. Even though the BT Graveyard was a spooky place, someone (probably the Headmaster herself) had tried to brighten this little area up. There were pillows scattered about and pictures of warm, exotic locales—Charlie recognized Hawaii as one of them. A chessboard sat on the floor next to the Guardian's bed, which was actually just a pile of blankets, and a game was in progress. Somehow, the effort to make the place look more cheerful had exactly the opposite effect: Charlie thought he'd never seen something so sad and lonely.

"Won't you hold me?" the Guardian asked again. "I would like to be held."

"It's so little," Violet said, walking toward the frail creature, arms outstretched. She desperately wanted to hug it and comfort it.

"It's dying, Ms. Sweet," the Headmaster said. "And if you touch it, you'll kill it."

Violet stopped, but it clearly took an enormous amount of willpower. There was just something about the frail being, something almost supernatural, that made you want to take it into your arms and protect it.

"Hold me," the Guardian pleaded. "Please . . . make me warm."

"That's enough, Hank," the Headmaster gently scolded. "You know they can't touch you. None of us can."

"Hank?" Theodore said with a laugh. "The Guardian's name is Hank?"

"I don't know what its actual name is," the Headmaster replied. "I'm not even sure it has one. But I used to have a dog named Hank that I liked very much, so . . ."

She shrugged, as if that said it all.

"You look kind," the Guardian whispered, turning to Brooke. "It would be okay if you held me, I think. I'm so cold and so lonely."

Brooke's eyes filled with tears. "What if I held it for just a second? Just a quick, little hug couldn't possibly—"

"Yes, it could, Ms. Brighton," the Headmaster snapped. "And it already has. One 'quick, little hug' is responsible for the Guardian being in the desperate condition you see now. This is exactly the reason why it must be protected from humans—the urge to touch it is nearly impossible to resist."

"Yes, Headmaster," Brooke said, turning away,

wiping tears from her eyes.

"So what happened?" Charlie asked. "Did someone touch it?"

The Headmaster nodded. "When I arrived, I found the Guardian in the arms of a child. The little girl was only trying to help, of course—as you were just now—but even the couple moments of contact she had with it have made it gravely ill."

"Where is she now?" Charlie asked. "The little girl."

"Home."

"How? I thought you couldn't open a portal here?"

"That's correct. I had to bring her out of range of the Anomaly to do so."

"To where the monsters are," Violet said softly.

"Indeed," the Headmaster replied. "There was . . . a certain amount of killing that had to be done, I'm afraid."

Charlie, who had seen the Headmaster in action, could easily imagine the amount of damage she had caused with her glowing blue staff. Once she got going, she was impossible to stop.

"Hold me," the Guardian whispered once more. "It's so dark in the Nether and I'm so frightened."

The urge to comfort the creature was enormous. Charlie didn't know how the Headmaster withstood it. He was already at the breaking point.

"Come outside," she said to them then. "And we will speak of things that need to be spoken."

They stood in the BT Graveyard, just out of earshot of the Guardian, although Charlie felt as if he could still hear every labored, rattling breath it took.

"If the Guardian dies," the Headmaster said, "the aura that it gives off will die with it, and it is that aura which repels the monsters of the Nether—in fact, it has soaked into the very ships that litter the ground here."

"That's what the Nightmare Academy is built out of, isn't it?" Charlie said, suddenly putting it all together. "Old ships from the BT Graveyard. That's why the Academy keeps away all the creatures of the Nether. The ships there hold the aura like a battery holds a charge."

"Precisely," the Headmaster said. "But only as long as the Guardian is *alive*. If it perishes, the Academy will be unprotected and the creatures of the Nether will overrun the BT Graveyard and escape to Earth."

"Then we have to save it!" Theodore exclaimed.

"Is there a way?" Charlie asked, trying hard to control his growing anxiety.

"There is," the Headmaster agreed, somewhat hesitantly. "That's why I asked Ms. Brighton to bring you here—but the danger is great, and success is by no means guaranteed."

"Well, I guarantee it," Theodore said. "There—you've got the Theodore Dagget Guarantee! Consider it done. What do we have to do?"

The Headmaster stared at them carefully, weighing their ability and resolve the way an expert tailor sizes up a customer and knows the right dimensions without taking a single measurement. Finally, she spoke: "There is a liquid in the Nether that is said to have astonishing restorative properties: one sip and you are returned to the point in your life when you were most powerful."

"Wow," Brooke said. "I'm guessing that's not easy to come by."

"You guess correctly."

"What is it?" Charlie asked.

"Milk," the Headmaster replied. "From a Hydra."

"A Hydra?" Theodore blurted. "You mean, a vicious multiheaded water dragon kind of Hydra?"

"Yes, but not just any Hydra—a female Hydra. Unfortunately, that's where the difficulty lies. There's only one female Hydra in existence, and we don't know where she is."

"So, to save the Guardian," Violet said, "we'd have to find the only female Hydra in the Nether, get her milk, and get it back to the Guardian before it dies."

"Precisely. And, at the rate the Guardian is slipping away, you have less than a day."

"No way!" Theodore exclaimed. "That's impossible!"

"Impossible?" the Headmaster replied. "But how can that be? I thought you guaranteed that it could be done."

"Well, that was before I actually knew what the job *was*. I mean, this is way more challenging than I thought it was gonna be."

"Well, I should hope so. It has the potential to save our world, so I'd be distrustful if it were easy."

"We'll do it," Charlie said quietly.

Everyone turned to him.

"Charlie?" Brooke said. "Are you sure?"

"Yeah. It needs to be done, that's all. There's no one else. The Headmaster has to stay here and protect the Guardian from other kids who might show up, and everyone in the Nightmare Division is hunting down Barakkas and Verminion. We'll do it because we have to."

He smiled confidently at Brooke.

"Wait a minute," Violet said, glancing between them. "Are you saying we'll do it because you want to impress *her*?"

Charlie flushed with embarrassment. "What? No! How can you even suggest that . . ."

"You *are*, aren't you? You're red as a beet!"

"Stop it!"

"Unbelievable. Seriously."

Charlie wished he could find a deep hole and bury himself in it. How could Violet accuse him of such a thing? There was no way he was doing this just to impress a girl!

Was there?

"Do you accept the task?" the Headmaster asked.

"Yes," Charlie said defiantly, then glanced at his friends. "Right?"

"You're the boss," Theodore replied quickly. "If you need me, I'm there, *mon frère*—that's French for 'my brother.' "

"Gotcha," Charlie said, then turned to Brooke. "So, you in?"

She gave him a quick smile. "Sure."

"Great!" He looked at Violet. "C'mon, Violet . . . please? I really need you. We *all* do."

She stared at him for a moment, then nodded grudgingly. "Okay."

"Good," the Headmaster said. "I'll walk you far enough away from the Anomaly so that you can portal out, and I'll keep the monsters off you while you do."

She strode away through the graveyard of wrecked ships. Charlie took one last look at the Guardian—so small, so fragile, so needy—then followed.

They walked in silence. The broken bodies of the ancient boats loomed around them like the ghosts of giants.

"There are likely more children stranded in the Nether," the Headmaster said after a time. "Keep an eye out for them. Rescue them if you can."

"We will," Charlie replied.

"But, above all, fulfill your mission. Nothing is as important. *Nothing.* Or I wouldn't have asked you to risk your lives."

She seemed gravely serious.

Soon, they left the protection of the Guardian's aura and headed toward the forest of razor-sharp, mustard-colored crystals that made up the rest of the 5th Ring. There was movement in them—shadowy things, dark and deadly.

"A few more yards, and you should be able to portal," the Headmaster said. She glanced disdainfully at Charlie's bent rapier and Violet's pitted dagger. "When you get to the Academy, outfit yourselves with new equipment. Those are Noob weapons."

"Does that mean we're Addys now?" Violet asked expectantly.

"Of course you are. Do you really think I'd send mere Noobs on a mission this dangerous?"

"Yes!" Theodore shouted, then turned to Charlie and raised his hand for a high-five. "Don't leave me hanging."

"Never." Charlie clapped him on the hand, all the while thinking that Pinch wasn't going to like their promotion very much.

"By the way," the Headmaster said, "would you please give a message from me to Mr. Pinch?" Charlie thought it was eerie how she almost seemed to read his mind.

"Sure."

"Please tell him he's no longer in charge of the Academy in my absence—that task now falls to Housemistress Rose. I want him to accompany you back to the Nether. I believe you'll find his experience . . . invaluable."

Charlie, Theodore, Brooke, and Violet glanced at one another unhappily.

"Yeah, right," Theodore muttered.

The Headmaster pretended she didn't hear.

Just then, a horrible shrieking filled the air, and Charlie clamped his hands over his ears—his eardrums felt like balloons filled to bursting. A hurricane-force wind blew down from the sky, and they all looked up to see a golden streak hurtling toward them from out of the swirling red pillar of the Inner Circle.

Charlie had seen that golden flash once before—in the crumbling manor of the Hags.

"Tyrannus," he said.

CHAPTER EIGHT

TYRANNUS THE DEMENTED

The enormous golden bat plummeted from the sky with the force of a tornado and slammed into the ground hard enough to shatter the massive crystals beneath its scaly feet. Its wingspan was gigantic—the width of a jumbo jet—and the slightest flutter from one of those wings was enough to knock down an elephant. It stared at the group with its wild, red eyes as it picked the remains of an Acidspitter from between pointy teeth with a claw that protruded from its wings. Around the bony finger, Charlie could see a ring, glittering blackly, with many carved images that issued red firelight.

That's one of the Artifacts of the Nether, he realized.

"GREETINGS and many great hellos!" the giant creature shrieked, bouncing up and down fifty yards from them, trampling several Nethercreatures that didn't move away quickly enough. "Welcome to this humble spot in the Nether. I am Tyrannus and it's a great pleasure to eat you!"

"Really?" the Headmaster shouted back. "If you're interested in eating us, why don't you come over here and do it?"

"Yum, yum—would be FUN!" Tyrannus said with a cackle. "But it's just so hard. The distance may be short, but the pain is loooong."

"Oh, you must mean from the Guardian's aura?" the Headmaster replied. "I forgot how horribly it affects you. I just *hate* that you can't go everywhere in the Nether that you'd like."

"Soon!" the great beast shouted cheerfully. "Soon the Guardian will be DEAD and I'll paint the ground RED with blood from . . ."

The Named creature suddenly stopped and cocked its head to the side, thinking.

"Your head?" Theodore offered. "That would rhyme. Paint the ground red with blood from your head? How about that?"

Charlie turned to him. "Are you crazy? Let the monster figure out its own rhymes, will ya?"

"Right," Theodore said, quickly nodding. "Sometimes I get a little caught up."

"I couldn't quite HEAR that," Tyrannus roared.

"Could you come a little closer, child, and whisper your rhyme in my ear . . . just so we're clear?"

"I think I'll pass," Theodore shouted back. "Or you'll knock me on my—"

"Mr. Dagget!" the Headmaster thundered, cutting him off. "Will you please let *me* handle this?"

"Right," Theodore said. "Definitely."

"What do you want, Tyrannus?" the Headmaster yelled to the creature. "We are busy people and don't have time to waste with you."

"To waste time suggests that there's a proper way to use time. I, personally, like to exercise my wings, eat the flesh of the innocent, and dance to the rhythm of the music in my head!"

The Named creature did a little jig. It shook the Nether like an earthquake.

Oh my God, Charlie thought. *He's insane!*

The Headmaster, seeing the realization in Charlie's eyes, shot him a look that said, quite clearly, *Be quiet.*

"Yes, we all like to dance a jig, now and again," she said, turning back to the great beast. "Is there some way we can help you?"

"Yes. I'd like to eat you."

"We can't allow that, I'm afraid. Is there anything else?"

"Yes. I have the bones of an Acidspitter stuck

between my teeth. Would you kindly climb inside my mouth and yank them out?"

"I would, but I have a sneaking suspicion that it might just be a clever ruse to eat us."

"Oh, you're TRICKY," Tyrannus roared with a sly grin. "Can't fool you! You're too sharp for old Tyrannus— sharp like a Hydra's tooth!"

"What is it you want?" the Headmaster asked, the playful tone now gone from her voice. "We have much to do."

"Oh, I *know*," Tyrannus replied. He suddenly became quite serious. "The Guardian is dying and you wish to save it. I, on the other hand, want that foul little beast dead. Therefore, I cannot permit you to leave."

"How, exactly, do you plan to stop us?"

"By killing you, of course. If you get far enough away from the Anomaly to portal out, you'll also be out of range of the Guardian's protection—and then I'll eat you."

He gave them a jolly wink.

"So, it's a standoff?" the Headmaster said.

"Only until the Guardian dies, and then it will be a 'head off,' as in I'll rip your heads off." Tyrannus smiled pleasantly. "So . . . how shall we pass the time?"

The Headmaster turned to Charlie and whispered,

"I'm about to do something and when I do, I want the rest of you to run out of range of the Anomaly and portal away."

"How will we know when it's time?"

The Headmaster's eyes twinkled. "Oh, you'll know. Now . . . get ready for the wetwash."

Suddenly, she ran forward, unprotected, straight at Tyrannus.

The reaction from the Named beast was instant.

The great creature rose up to his full height and fanned out his wings. From this close, their size was staggering. He let out a screech that dropped Charlie to his knees, but the Headmaster didn't falter. She continued to run toward the monster—looking, for all the world, like a mouse attacking a lion.

She's gonna die, Charlie thought. *There's no way she can survive this.*

Tyrannus rushed toward her. A heartbeat before they made contact, the Headmaster waved her hand, and a giant portal snapped open between them. Ocean water roared out of it with such force that it knocked Tyrannus backward, causing him to tumble end over end in a tangle of wings, washing away the Class-5 creatures that tried to come to his aid.

She opened a portal to the middle of Earth's ocean, Charlie realized. Now he understood what the term "wetwash" meant: It was a last resort, designed to clear away everything when the odds were too long and escape was the only thing that mattered.

"Come on!" he shouted to his friends. "Let's do it!"

They all ran toward Tyrannus, trying to get out of range of the Anomaly as the Named beast struggled to regain its footing. Every instinct in Charlie told him to run away from the deadly creature, not at it, but he knew that the chance the Headmaster had given them was the only chance they were likely to get.

As he ran, he extended his right hand, closed his eyes, and tried to open a portal. Usually it was easy, but not this close to the Anomaly. He could feel its alien power smothering him like a wet blanket on an ember. He focused harder, trying desperately to access his personal fear: the dread of being an outcast, alone in a world that despised him.

I've led my friends into danger for nothing, he thought. *And why? To impress a girl? How could I be so stupid? They're gonna die because of me, and then I'll be left here, all alone. . . .*

Alone.

To Charlie's great relief, that ember of fear started to grow into a brightly burning flame. As he ran toward Tyrannus, he could feel the power of the Anomaly begin to lessen, and moments later he opened a portal back to the Nightmare Academy.

"You did it!" Brooke yelled and Charlie flushed again with embarrassment—embarrassed that she had singled him out like that and embarrassed that it meant so much to him that she did.

With one flap of his giant wings, Tyrannus rose into the air above the powerful stream of water from the Headmaster's portal, then dived at Charlie and his friends with a hideous, brain-melting screech . . . but by the time he got to them, they were gone.

They had returned to the Nightmare Academy.

The armory of the Nightmare Academy was located in the large hold of an iron frigate near the base of the banyan tree, where the branches were thicker and could support the massive weight of the metal ship. Charlie and Violet inspected the many rows of weapons that were hung on hooks under a sign marked ADDY GEAR.

"They're all definitely nicer than the Noob weapons," Charlie said. "But I still kind of like my rapier."

He swished it deftly through the air to make his point.

"I hear you," Violet said. "I still like Bun-Bun—he's my stuffed bunny from when I was a little girl—but sometimes you have to know when it's time to say good-bye, you know? How would that little rapier protect you against something like Tyrannus?"

"How would *anything* protect us against a monster like him?"

"Let's go!" a stern voice behind them commanded. "This is just an upgrade. It ain't like you gotta marry it."

Charlie was happy to hear the rough but somehow welcoming sound of Mama Rose's voice. She was a large woman, pink-cheeked and strong, and she gave off an aura of comfort like the smell of home-baked chocolate-chip cookies.

Mama Rose turned to Violet. "Go on. Look around, girlie, and find one that speaks to you."

Violet looked over the many spears and maces and swords that were precisely mounted on the iron wall. In a way, it reminded Charlie of how his dad used to hang tools in the garage. Suddenly, her eyes lit up.

"That one," she said, pointing. It was a one-handed ax with a double-sided blade as long as her forearm, and a handle made of ash.

Mama Rose grinned. "It's talking to ya, ain't it?"

"Oh, yeah."

"Then take it."

Violet lifted the weapon from its hook. Holding it easily in her right hand, she gave the ax a few casual swipes through the air.

"Wow—it feels light but strong."

"A big step up from that puny little dagger, huh, girlie?"

"Absolutely! It makes me feel powerful just holding it."

"That's how a Banisher *should* feel."

"I don't know why *I* can't pick out a weapon," Theodore moaned. He had been standing in the corner, pouting. "Sure, maybe I wouldn't be a hundred percent as good as Violet and Charlie, but I know how to handle one. I come from a long line of Banishers, you know."

"That so?" Mama Rose said mildly, then turned to Violet. "Why don't you give him yours?"

"My new ax?"

"Sure. Hand it over to him. He said he can handle it."

"Fine," Violet said, clearly reluctant, but she did as Mama Rose told her.

"Come to Daddy!" Theodore said gleefully, wrapping his fist around the ax handle—but the second Violet let go of it, the weapon clanged to the ground with the force of an anvil.

Mama Rose laughed, long and loud.

"Good grief!" Theodore shouted. "It's so heavy!

How can you even lift it?"

"I don't know," Violet said with a shrug. "It doesn't feel heavy to me."

"Because you're a Banisher, girlie!" Mama Rose said. "That's the way it's supposed to feel to you." She turned to Theodore. "And when are you gonna stop tryin' to be something you're not, little mister?"

Theodore, embarrassed and angry, stomped out of the armory without saying a word.

"You shouldn't have done that," Charlie said. "You really hurt his feelings."

Mama Rose swiveled her large head toward him. The look in her eye made Charlie wish he'd never said a word. "Now, you listen to me, Charlie Benjamin, and you listen *good*. You ain't doing that boy any favors by coddlin' him and tellin' him he's something he's not. He can either be a great Nethermancer or a crappy Banisher. It may not seem like it now, but that can make the difference between him being a hero and him being dead. You wanna be responsible for that?"

"No, ma'am," Charlie said quietly.

"Then grow up."

Grow up. The two words hung in the air like a poisonous cloud.

Desperate to escape it, Charlie turned back to the

wall of weapons and searched for something to replace his rapier. After a moment, he spotted just the thing.

"Another rapier?" Violet said in disbelief as Charlie took down the shiny new sword. It cut through the air with a satisfying *swish*.

"Well, if it ain't broke . . ."

"There's our new little Addy," a voice behind them said. Charlie turned to see Pinch approach. "I see it didn't take you long to go over my head to get precisely what you wanted."

Oh boy, Charlie thought. *Here it comes.*

"The Headmaster told us to upgrade our weapons," Violet replied, stepping in front of Charlie. "That's why she made us Addys. We didn't ask her to do it."

"Oh, I'm sure," Pinch said wryly. "You're completely innocent, just like every convict in every penitentiary—*not guilty* to the very last man. So, Theodore tells me we have a little adventure ahead of us, led by young master Benjamin."

"The Headmaster wanted you to join us in our quest to get Hydra milk," Charlie said, "because of your knowledge of the Nether."

"Yes, my knowledge is vast and deep, just like the ocean of the 4th Ring—which is, coincidentally, exactly where we are headed. Shall we go?"

Charlie, Pinch, Theodore, and Violet assembled on the deck of the pirate ship to prepare for their return to the Nether.

"I may have to open a couple of portals to find the 4th Ring," Charlie said. "It could take a bit of trial and error because I've never portaled there before."

"Well, I have," Theodore said cheerfully.

They all stared at him in disbelief.

"What? Okay, yes, it was a mistake and yes, I almost got eaten—but you can't make an omelet without breaking a few eggs, right?"

"Sounds like you broke the whole carton," Violet said with a grin.

"Ha-ha. Good news is, I can get us back there—no worries."

Amazingly, he was already over his anger about Mama Rose's comment. Charlie was astonished at how easily Theodore changed his moods. Emotions for him were like a storm that crept up without warning and blew away just as quickly.

"Hey, sorry I'm late!"

They turned to see Brooke arriving in a dinghy. She had changed clothes and brushed her hair. Every time Charlie thought she'd gotten as pretty as she could get, she surprised him by looking even prettier.

"Hey, Brooke!" Theodore said, bounding toward her. "You're right on time."

"Why is she coming?" Violet asked, clearly aggravated. "I mean—no offense, Brooke—but you're not a Banisher or a Nethermancer."

"True," she replied, somewhat defensively. "But I'm a Leet Facilitator. I may know some things that are helpful."

"Absolutely, and that's why Professor Pinch is going." Violet turned to the bearded man. "Right?"

Pinch grinned, seeming to enjoy the conflict between the kids like a starving man before a great and wonderful feast.

"I think," Pinch began pleasantly, "that we should let Charlie decide if Brooke should join us or not. After all, the Headmaster, in her great wisdom, put him in charge of this little adventure, so he should make the call, shouldn't he?"

Everyone turned to Charlie. He shifted his weight uncomfortably.

"Well?" Violet said. "Is she going?"

"Um . . ."

"Do you *want* me to go, Charlie?" Brooke asked, leaning toward him. Her nearness was unsettling and thrilling, all at the same time.

"Have fun with this one!" Theodore said, laughing.

"All I can say is, this is the first time I'm glad I'm not you."

Charlie hated to do it, but clearly a choice had to be made. If he said yes, then Violet would claim it was because he had a crush on Brooke and was trying to impress her. But if he said no, then Brooke would say it was because he was Violet's little puppet and did whatever she told him to do. It was a no-win situation.

Should he upset Violet or upset Brooke?

"I think," he said after a moment's careful consideration, "that it might be best for you to stay here, Brooke, and take care of our home base. I mean, it's gonna be pretty dangerous and there's no need to risk all of our lives unnecessarily, right?"

Brooke stared at him, clearly crushed and angry.

"Right," she said finally. "Good luck, everyone."

She turned, stepped back into the waiting dinghy, and quickly descended into the leafy branches below. Violet seemed very pleased, but Charlie wanted to die.

Not smooth, he thought. *Not smooth at all.*

"Well!" Pinch exclaimed, greatly amused. "Let's head into the Nether and get that milk, shall we?"

· CHAPTER NINE ·
THE TERRIFYING OCEAN

Rex had once referred to the ocean on the 4th Ring as "the Chill Depths." As usual, Pinch had argued with him, saying that he preferred to call it "the Terrifying Ocean." Rex quickly dismissed the bearded man's suggestion, saying that the name lacked beauty and poetry, but seeing the ocean now for the first time, Charlie thought that Pinch had it exactly right—it *was* terrifying.

So vast he couldn't see to the end of it, the ocean of the 4th Ring was an eternity of water, rough and black and cold. High waves crashed at the shoreline in front of them in a stinging spray. The whitecaps were a dingy gray color, and the raw wind that whipped off the water's surface had an unpleasant smell of rot.

"This place sucks," Theodore said, looking around in dismay.

"Totally," Charlie replied. He turned to Pinch. "So, what do you think we should do?"

"Me?" Pinch said in mock surprise. "You want my opinion? But I'm not the leader of this merry little band—you are."

"C'mon, don't be like that," Charlie pressed. "We need your help. I don't have a clue how to find this Mother Hydra."

Pinch shook his head. "No, no, no—that's impossible. The Headmaster put you in charge, so you must know what do. After all, if she thought I was the right person for the job, she would have put me in charge."

Charlie sighed. He knew Pinch could be a pain, but this was more than he had bargained for.

"We should've brought Brooke," Theodore muttered. "She may not know as much, but at least she would've told us what she *did* know."

"Excellent point!" Pinch grinned at Charlie. "What a shame: your very first decision as leader and already your followers are doubting your judgment. I wonder if the Headmaster was wrong in picking you to lead us after all."

"Knock it off," Violet said. "This isn't about you or us, it's about doing what's right, so do what's right and help us!"

Charlie wasn't quite sure if Violet really meant it or if she just didn't want to be wrong about leaving Brooke behind. Either way, it seemed to work.

"Hydras prefer deep water," Pinch said finally. "Which is why we won't see any of them here at the shore."

"Okay, good," Charlie replied. "So we just need to find a way to get out into the middle of the ocean."

"I could open a portal," Theodore suggested. "Then we could steal a boat."

"Great, how?"

"I don't know how!" Theodore said. "I'm just the idea man, the dude with the overview, the guy who thinks about the big picture. You have to figure out the logistics."

"Me? Why do I always have to—"

"Look over there," Violet said before Charlie could finish. She pointed to what looked like a silvery raft bobbing in the water, just beyond the break line. "What is that?"

"That," Pinch said with a slight smile, "is the solution to our first little problem."

It wasn't a raft. It was a jellyfish.

A giant jellyfish.

Charlie fought his way through the pounding waves to where the silvery creature floated in the dark, freezing water.

"Be careful of the tentacles!" Pinch shouted, as he and the others followed. "If you get stung, the poison will paralyze you."

Great, Charlie thought, staring down into the murky water. *Leave it to us to pick the only raft that can paralyze you.*

He could see a tangle of glowing tentacles drifting below the large creature. Thick and long, they pulsed sickly until they disappeared, squirming, into the darkness. Careful to avoid them, Charlie grabbed onto the jellyfish's rubbery back and climbed on top. It felt disgusting—like a sticky, wet slug—and he could see its organs beating gently below its shiny, translucent skin.

"Ugh, this is pretty gross," Violet said, climbing up after him. "So what do you call these things?"

"Bang-Jellies," Pinch said, as Violet pulled him up.

"Bang-Jellies?" Theodore repeated, scrambling onto the back of the creature, as well. "What kinda stupid name is Bang-Jellies?"

"An appropriate one, trust me."

"Okay," Charlie said. "So how do we get this Bang-Jelly to take us where we want to go?"

"Easy, really. They're simple, instinctive creatures.

They either propel themselves toward food or away from harm."

"Perfect," Violet said, walking to the side of the Bang-Jelly nearest the shore. She took out her ax and poked the creature with a corner of the blade.

The reaction was instantaneous.

The Bang-Jelly quickly began floating away from shore—and the sting of Violet's weapon—toward the deep, dark water beyond. Charlie was surprised by Violet's cold efficiency. He would have done the same thing, probably, but it would have bothered him to do it.

"Sweet!" Theodore exclaimed as the Bang-Jelly carried them out into the open ocean. "Now we just gotta keep our eyes peeled for a Hydra."

A half hour later, they spotted one.

It was navigating through a giant school of Bang-Jellies that were floating on the dark water like bobbers. Charlie was surprised by how large the Hydra was. The size of a bulldozer, it had six heads, all with shiny, sharp teeth. Its green, scaly hide made it look something like a dragon with a wide tail that propelled it forward through the choppy waves.

"Is that the female?" Charlie asked.

Pinch shook his head. "Wrong size, wrong color. The female is much bigger and bluish in color, or so it is rumored. No one has ever seen it, of course, which is why we don't know where it is."

Suddenly, the Hydra let out a howl of pain. It began to thrash, kicking up large sheets of ocean water. Around its paddle-like feet, Charlie could see glowing tentacles stuck to it in great spaghetti-like mounds.

"That Bang-Jelly's got him!" Violet said. "And the others are moving toward it!"

"So is ours," Charlie added, noticing that their Bang-Jelly was homing in on the struggling Hydra.

As the Bang-Jellies surrounded the writhing creature, it became entangled in their poisonous tentacles—the harder it struggled, the more hopelessly wrapped up it was. The Hydra snapped violently at its attackers with all six of its heads, successfully tearing open large gashes that oozed a thick, clear fluid.

"Hey!" Theodore shouted. "Look, they're turning red!"

Sure enough, every Bang-Jelly fighting the Hydra was slowly changing color from silver to a deep scarlet that glowed brightly from within.

"Uh-oh," Pinch said softly.

"What?" Charlie demanded. "What 'uh-oh'?"

"Perhaps you'd better steer us away from them."

"Why?"

One of the Bang-Jellies suddenly exploded with such immense force that it nearly ripped the six-headed

Hydra in half. One by one, in a nightmarish chain reaction, all the Bang-Jellies began to explode with thunderous crashes, each as loud as cannon fire. Great gouts of flesh and goo rained down on Charlie and his friends.

"That's why," Pinch said, pulling sticky bits of flesh from his beard.

As they neared the exploding creatures, Charlie dashed to the front of their Bang-Jelly and jabbed his rapier into it, hard. The creature moved in the opposite direction, away from the other Bang-Jellies.

"C'mon, c'mon . . . ," Charlie urged.

Their Bang-Jelly drifted away from the explosions with agonizing slowness, and Charlie was sure they were going to get caught in the last wave of creatures to detonate—but they managed to sail just out of range before the final one blew up in a disgusting, violent spray.

"Nasty," Violet said as they wiped chunks of meat and ooze from their faces.

"Nasty? That was awesome!" Theodore shouted. "What a show!"

"I admit it was pretty spectacular," Charlie said. "But it doesn't make any sense. They intentionally kill themselves to take down opponents? That's crazy."

"Bees do it," Pinch said. "After a bee stings you, it

dies, because a single bee doesn't matter—only the swarm. The same is true of the Bang-Jellies. They sacrifice the individual to protect the group."

"I guess."

"You guess? Do you think I'm lying to you? Do you think I've just gone insane and decided to spend my day feeding you misinformation like some kind of lunatic?"

"No," Charlie replied, taken aback by Pinch's weird outburst. "I'm just saying it doesn't seem like a very good survival strategy."

"And what do you know about survival?" Pinch roared, clearly getting angrier by the second. "Nothing terrible has happened to you! You've had nothing to overcome—your parents are still alive, you've still got the Gift, and you're here acting like you know more than me when I was once the greatest that ever was! My power was so strong that you would have looked like a fool in comparison, Charlie Benjamin—you miserable, arrogant little *child*!"

Whoa, where did that come from? Charlie wondered.

Theodore and Violet glanced uncomfortably at each other. Neither knew quite how to respond.

"I'm sorry," Charlie said finally. He figured it must be pretty tough for a proud man like Pinch to have to answer to a thirteen-year-old. "I know you lost your parents when you were our age, and I know it wasn't right what the Division did to you all those years ago. I never meant to question you. I was just—"

"What? You were just what?"

Charlie was about to answer when he felt an odd swell beneath his feet. "Did anyone else just feel that?"

"I did," Violet said, alarmed.

Charlie looked over the side of their Bang-Jelly and peered into the dark water below. It was like looking into an inkwell.

"I guess it was nothing. It just felt like—"

A Hydra exploded up from the depths and crashed down on top of their Bang-Jelly, capsizing it. Everyone fell into the murky water of the 4th Ring. The multi-headed creature tried to swim after them, teeth snapping, but it was quickly entangled in a gooey mess of stinging tentacles from the now upside-down Bang-Jelly.

"Swim!" Charlie shouted. "Get away! It's gonna blow!"

Sure enough, their former raft began to glow a brilliant red.

They swam frantically away from the Bang-Jelly as the Hydra tore into it, but the more it fought, the more it got twisted up in those paralyzing stingers. Soon, the two creatures were an undifferentiated mass of teeth and tentacles and thick, spraying ooze.

"Keep going!" Charlie screamed, spitting rank, salty water from his mouth. "Just a few feet more! I think we're almost in the clea—"

The Bang-Jelly exploded, killing the Hydra instantly and sending a massive shock wave through the water. It hit Theodore with such force that it knocked him unconscious.

He began to slip into the black, fathomless depths.

"Theodore!" Charlie yelled, trying desperately to stay afloat himself. The water was freezing and his muscles were beginning to seize up. He swam toward where Theodore had gone under, but he was still many yards away.

"I got him!" Violet yelled, and dived down into the murk.

Find him, Charlie thought with growing panic. *Please, don't let him die.*

He counted seventeen endless seconds before, to his great relief, Violet burst back above the surface, holding an unconscious Theodore against her chest.

"Wake up, Theo!" she shouted. "I can't get a good grip on you!"

Theodore's eyes fluttered open. "Are we there yet?"

"No, we're nowhere," Charlie shouted back, treading water. "We're alone in the middle of the ocean on the 4th Ring of the Nether!"

"Not alone," Pinch said, staring grimly into the distance. "Not anymore."

Charlie looked up to see another Hydra rapidly approaching them. "Great," he muttered, drawing his rapier.

Within moments, the beast arrived and snapped at him with its six sets of pointy teeth. Charlie felt a familiar feeling of calm wash over him as his Banishing skill took over. He fended off attack after attack from those vicious jaws with a speed and grace that seemed almost supernatural—and, in fact, *was*—but he knew he couldn't keep it up for forever.

If only I could open a portal, he thought. *Then the water would rush through and take us all out of here with it!*

But, even though he was a Double-Threat and could both Banish and Nethermance, he knew he couldn't do both at the same time. If he stopped fighting for even a second to open a portal, he and everyone else would surely die. Theodore was too weak to help, and it took all of Violet's strength just to keep Theodore from drowning. And Pinch . . . well, it had been decades since he had been able to open a portal—the Nightmare Division's repulsive process of Reduction had stolen that from him.

Charlie was still swinging his rapier to ward off the Hydra when he noticed two more of the vicious beasts swimming toward them.

Now there were three.

"Stop fighting!" Pinch shouted. "You can't win this!"

"What?" Charlie yelled back. "Are you crazy? If I stop fighting, they'll eat me. They'll eat *all* of us!"

"Just do what I tell you!"

"That's suicide."

"Listen to me or you will die! Now put . . . your weapon . . . down!"

What is he talking about? Charlie thought. Had Pinch just given up? Did he just want to end it all?

"Listen to him!" a voice called out from somewhere behind Charlie. It was Violet. "We can't beat them anyway! Do what he says—we don't have a choice!"

Fighting every instinct in his body, Charlie lowered his rapier.

The moment he did, one of the Hydra's mouths clamped down over him, swallowing him up to his waist. He could feel its sharp teeth pressing against his back and belly. It was wet in there and as black as a closed coffin. Charlie could smell the stink of the creature's previous meal drifting up from its stomach—it smelled like spoiled fish and rotten seaweed.

So this is how I die, he thought. *This is how we* all *die.*

An image of his parents appeared to him then, smiling kindly, always loving. He hadn't seen them in months—the Nightmare Division had hidden them away somewhere and given them new names and identities to protect them from the monsters of the Nether.

He wished he knew where they were and if they were happy and safe.

He wished he could hug them one more time.

He wished—

But then the darkness took him.

· CHAPTER TEN ·
TO MILK A HYDRA

Charlie awoke to find himself lying on a large pile of bones at the bottom of a deep pit. Water dripped from the ceiling high above, and he could hear streams of it flowing on either side. He glanced over to see the others next to him, also beginning to stir. He had no idea where they were, exactly—some kind of cave, it looked like—but he knew they were alive, at least, and that was the most important thing. He lifted his shirt to find that the Hydra's teeth had left pinpricks of blood across his stomach and back but, thankfully, the damage was no worse than that.

"Charlie . . . ," a weak voice called out beside him. It was Violet. "Did we all make it?"

"I think so . . . but I don't know how. Why didn't the Hydra eat us?"

"It's because of their social structure," Pinch said, raising himself up and propping his elbows on the bony spine of some kind of giant fish—bits of meat still clung to its ribcage. "None of the workers are allowed to eat before the Mother Hydra does—she gets first pick of all the food. Once she's done, the males can have what's left."

"So that's why you told me to stop fighting and let them take us?" Charlie asked. "You knew that they'd bring us to the Mother Hydra?"

Pinch shrugged. "Well, it was worth a try, wasn't it? I think we should all just be thankful that she likes her meals alive when she eats them, or our circumstances would truly be dire."

"You mean more dire than being trapped in a Hydra nest waiting to get eaten by the Queen?" Theodore asked, sitting up.

"Dire is better than *dead*, Mr. Dagget. Wouldn't you agree?"

"I'd agree that my butt hurts from lying on all these bones."

"Okay," Violet said. "Let's see what we're up against." She clambered to the lip of the pit. Charlie followed, but what he saw once he got there wasn't encouraging. They were in some kind of underwater cave. Rivers of water fed large, dark pools. Male Hydras dived in and out of them, presumably to swim out to the ocean beyond. There had to be at least thirty of the wretched beasts. Just past the pools, Charlie got his first glimpse of the Mother Hydra, lounging like a queen upon her throne.

She was enormous, nearly the size of a whale. Her brilliant blue scales shone brightly even in the dim light of the cavern. A couple of her large, toothy heads kept watch while the rest of them slept peacefully by her side. A few adventurous baby Hydras, each the size of a bear, playfully wrestled with one another throughout the cave while the rest crowded around her, nursing at the many ducts that ran up and down her plated belly.

"You see those ducts?" Violet said, pointing at the Mother Hydra's stomach. "That's where we get the milk."

"Right," Charlie said. "Perfect."

"Perfect?" Theodore repeated as he scrambled up out of the pit next to them. "What do you mean, *perfect*? How are we gonna *get* the milk? This isn't a supermarket. We can't just walk up and buy a quart!"

"Shhh!" Charlie and Violet said at the same time.

"Look, Theodore," Violet continued. "Finding the Mother Hydra was the hardest part. Now one of us just has to sneak over there and milk her."

"Oh, is *that* all?" Theodore whispered. "Just sneak

up and milk the giant monster? Easy!"

A couple of the nearby baby Hydras turned and looked at them.

"Shhhh!" Charlie and Violet said again, more forcefully this time.

"You don't have to worry about it," Charlie added, "because I'm the one who's gonna go do it."

"Negatory," Theodore replied. "This operation requires skill and subtlety, exactly the kind of procedure that Dr. Dagget performs—the Doctor of Gettin' It Done! I'm all man, baby! That's just the way I roll."

"Uh-huh," Charlie said, grinning. "Well, tempting as that offer is, you've got to stay back here to portal everyone out in case something goes wrong."

"Like what? You die?"

"Theodore!" Violet snapped.

"Hey, don't look at me—he brought it up!"

"I'm not gonna die," Charlie said. "I just mean . . . there's a lot here we can't control."

"Which could lead to you *dying*," Theodore repeated. "Which is why I'm doing this and you're not."

"The decision is made." Charlie turned away from him as if that settled it.

"Ah, the decision is made. Okay. Gotcha. So is there anything in particular you'd like me to tell your parents if things don't work out with this great decision? And how would you like us to handle your remains? For instance, if there's just a finger left, do you want us to retrieve it for the funeral or would you prefer a closed casket?"

"Theodore, that's sick!"

"And it's not gonna work," Charlie added. "You're not gonna scare me. I'm doing this."

"What about me?" Violet said, "I can do it. Or am I out of the running because I'm a girl?" Her stare was withering.

"Look, I know you can do it," Charlie said. "But you have to stay back here to keep the Hydras off Theodore while he makes a portal in case something goes wrong. Basically, I need you here to fight."

"I can fight," Theodore said. "She's not the only one who can fight, you know, just 'cause she's a Banisher."

Charlie closed his eyes tightly.

"You guys are making me crazy, you know that? Will you both please just stay here and handle things on this end without a gigantic argument so I can go milk the Mother Hydra in peace?"

"Sure," Violet said.

"Good. Theodore?"

"What? Yes! Just go milk your stupid Hydra. Geez."

"Do you have a plan, at least?" Violet asked. "I mean, how do you think you're gonna get across all that open ground without being spotted?"

"I'll show you." Charlie turned to the nearest baby Hydra and called out to it: "Hey there, little fella."

The baby Hydra's six heads swiveled toward him. *It's actually kind of cute in a crazy way,* Charlie thought. He continued sweet-talking to it. "That's a good baby. Come over here, nice little Hydra. Come to Charlie."

The baby looked at him quizzically, then stumbled toward him on its four unsteady legs.

"What a good boy!" Charlie whispered. "Here, Hydra, Hydra, Hydra . . . here, cute baby Hydra . . ."

"Well, that's not something you hear every day," Theodore said. "Out of curiosity, what makes you think the baby won't want to, you know, eat you? It may be an infant, but it's still twice your size."

"It won't eat me because it doesn't eat meat yet. It's still drinking mother's milk, which means it should take me straight to the mother."

After a couple of seconds, the baby Hydra arrived, and Charlie gently stroked one of its six heads. It cooed, seeming to like the attention.

"Okay, here we go."

Charlie glanced at the adult male Hydras that were busily shuffling around the large cavern. They seemed unaware of what was happening, so he quickly jumped out of the pit and slithered underneath the monstrous infant. He wrapped his arms and legs around it, clinging to its belly like a baby monkey.

"Let's go, little fella. Let's go to Mommy. Aren't you hungry? Aren't you thirsty?"

The baby just stood there. Charlie couldn't figure out why it wasn't moving until he realized that it was staring curiously at Theodore.

"Goo-goo-goo!" the skinny boy said to the baby monster. "You are a little six-headed mutant! You are a scaly little freak!" He put his thumbs in his ears, wiggled his fingers, and stuck out his tongue while making a raspberry noise.

"Theodore?" Charlie said through gritted teeth, still desperately clinging to the underside of the creature.

"Yeah?"

"Will you please . . . stop distracting . . . the monster."

"Oh, sure thing."

Without another word, Theodore slid down into the pit to join Pinch in the tangle of bones.

"Good luck," Violet said. "You either be real careful or real lucky."

"I'll try to be both." He gave her a quick smile, then turned to the baby Hydra. "Come on, little fella. Let's go see Mommy."

The baby Hydra turned and headed through the vast cavern while Charlie clung to its belly. As it weaved uncertainly through the adult male Hydras, Charlie held his breath, praying that none of them would see him or smell him. To his relief, not a single beast even glanced in his direction.

Finally, the infant arrived at its mother.

From this close, her stomach looked like a cliff face, tall and hard and sheer. Charlie could hear the babies suckling as they crowded around the many rows of milk-giving ducts.

Just relax, he told himself. *Be still.*

Luckily, the babies were too interested in feeding to notice him. As for the Mother Hydra, four of her heads were asleep and the two that remained awake had heavy-lidded eyes and looked as if they might nod off at any time. As Charlie's baby Hydra began to suckle, he slid out from underneath it and, searching quickly, found an unused duct that wept a thin white fluid.

Milk! he thought gleefully. *Hydra milk—finally!*

Then—to his complete horror—he realized that in all the craziness he hadn't brought anything to put the Hydra milk *in.*

Oh, no, he thought. *How could I have forgotten something so simple? Stupid! Stupid!*

He forced himself to calm down and think. There

must be something he had, some little container that that would work, right? He frantically inspected everything on him: belt, shoes, wallet? No, no, and no.

C'mon!

The more he searched, the less he seemed to find until, suddenly, success—

Chapstick.

In his pocket was a little tube of grape, Flava-Craze Chapstick.

He took it out, popped off the cap, and spun the dial until the waxy stuff inside was completely exposed. Then he threw the innards away, leaving himself with a small, cylindrical container and a cap.

Thank heaven, he thought, sweating profusely. *That should do it.* After all, the Headmaster had said that the Guardian only needed a sip, didn't she? The Chapstick container should hold more than enough.

Forcing himself to focus despite his frantically beating heart, he turned back to the weeping duct—

—only to find himself face to face with one of the Mother Hydra's heads.

The great beast's lips drew back to reveal black gums that held crooked teeth as long as baseball bats. Her orange eyes drew down to snakelike slits and she stared at him with silent fury.

"Oh no," Charlie gasped. "This can't be happening."

"How's Charlie doing?" Theodore asked.

"It's hard to tell," Violet replied, looking intently. "There's so many babies crawling around over there that I can't really even see him."

Just then, the Mother Hydra roared loudly enough that the sound waves caused violent ripples to form in the still pools. The great beast leaped to her feet, all six heads awake and snapping furiously.

"Run!" they heard a voice cry out then—it was Charlie. "Portal away! Mayday! Mayday!"

The little figure of Charlie Benjamin came running toward them from across the cavern floor, but he was still almost a football field away.

"How did I know this was going to happen?" Pinch moaned, as adult Hydras descended on them from all sides in a forest of chomping jaws. Violet's ax seemed to spring into her hands so fast that it looked like a magician's trick. With a few quick swipes of its glowing blue blade, several Hydra heads dropped down into the pit, twitching wildly.

"Open a portal!" Violet yelled to Theodore. "And I'll hold them off you as long as I can!"

She began to spin, bobbing up and down with her double-bladed ax, lopping off monster heads as she did. Theodore, meanwhile, closed his eyes and tried to access his core fear—

If I die in here, he thought, *my dad will kill me.*

Charlie sprinted through the cavern like a man who . . . well, like a man who had a giant Hydra chasing after him. He lifted the closed Chapstick container to his ear and gave it a quick shake.

There was a slight sloshing sound in there.

Milk.

Hydra milk.

Just before the deadly beast attacked, he'd managed to steal one quick squeeze of milk from the duct nearest him. *It's not much,* he thought, *but hopefully it will be enough.*

Even though his tremendous skill as a Banisher gave him unnatural speed, the Mother Hydra quickly gained on him, the hot breath from her mouths blasting his back like a furnace. He knew he couldn't outrun her or outfight her, so his only option was to outthink her.

"Catch!" Charlie yelled and threw the Chapstick container across the cavern and into the waiting hands of Pinch.

"Got it!" Pinch shouted back, ducking the jaws of one Hydra while getting saved from another by Violet's astonishing ax work. While Theodore tried to open his portal, Charlie got ready to open a different one—this time to the Pacific Ocean.

Wetwash, he thought. *Time for the last resort.*

Running frantically, he extended his right hand, closed his eyes, and started to open a portal—

—but, before he could finish, the ground began to rumble violently.

Stalactites plunged from the ceiling and slammed into the rock below like massive spears. The water from the many pools sloshed over their banks, creating a slick surface that Charlie and the Hydras skidded across wildly.

What's happening? he thought.

There was something familiar about the shaking, about the way the ground was moving. . . .

No, he thought. *It can't be!*

The rocky floor in the center of the chamber exploded upward, and a gigantic wormlike creature sailed out of it. Its massive, gray body was as thick as a rocket and seemed nearly as long. Hundreds of legs lined its sides, like a centipede, and its head was a pointed dome that looked for all the world like a giant drill bit. The creature hovered high in the air, curled in an *S* shape, until the hard dome of its head peeled back to expose two large, dark eyes and a buglike face with waving antennae.

Midway down its body was a shiny black belt, covered in red runes. Charlie immediately recognized it as one of the Artifacts of the Nether.

"Hello, Charlie Benjamin," the Named Lord said in a voice choked with dirt.

"Hello, Slagguron," Charlie replied.

· CHAPTER ELEVEN ·
SLAGGURON THE UNCHANGING

"Y ou know who I am?" the Third Named asked. His thunderous voice caused tremors throughout the cavern.

"Well, I've met the other Named, and you're wearing one of the Artifacts of the Nether"—Charlie pointed to the glowing belt around Slagguron's oozing middle—"plus you're the size of a building, so I just made an educated guess."

"I had heard you were smart, Charlie Benjamin. Quick. To be respected." Slagguron smiled. "I heard correctly."

"Well, you may have heard about me, but I haven't heard much about you. Near as I can tell, no one's ever even seen you."

"I stay underground. Alone. Unlike the others." Slagguron said the word *others* with a hint of distaste.

"You don't like them?" Charlie asked. He figured that any rift among the Named could be used to his advantage in the future—if he lived to *see* the future.

"I don't like or dislike them. I am one of Four. I serve my purpose."

"To summon the Fifth?"

The great creature nodded. "To do what I must, I need your help, Charlie Benjamin. You must open a portal to bring me to Earth."

"I thought you had a different plan." Charlie began to walk toward him. "I thought you were using children to kill the Guardian, and then you were planning to escape through the Anomaly."

"No. That is Tyrannus's plan. The Anomaly is too high for me to reach. I cannot fly."

Charlie was a little taken aback—that had never even occurred to him. "I guess you can't. So you didn't scheme to bring those children to the Nether?"

Slagguron shook his head. "They do not belong here."

"Trust me," Charlie said, "we're not going to leave any of them behind. Any kids we find, we're taking straight back to Earth."

"Take me with them." Slagguron's voice was steady and calm, as if he were asking nothing more challenging of Charlie than to give him a quick ride on his bike to the 7-Eleven.

"You can't really believe I'd do that, do you? I mean, that would be crazy. You're planning to kill us."

"Yes."

"So why would I ever help you?"

Slagguron slithered forward—it was like a sky-scraper moving. "We four Named will get to Earth, Charlie Benjamin. With you or without you. Join me and you will be respected. Protected."

"That's a lie. Barakkas told me the same thing, and then he tried to kill me. Verminion said the same to Pinch before he slaughtered his whole family."

"That's right," Pinch said from somewhere far behind Charlie.

Slagguron flicked a look his way. Pinch quickly retreated.

"That is true," the monster said, "but do not compare me with the others. Verminion is a liar. He says one thing but means another. His words shift. They change. I am unchanging, like the rock I burrow through."

"What about Barakkas?" Charlie prompted. "What do you think about him?"

"One moment he is normal, the next he rages. He is not steady. He changes. I am unchanging, like the rock I burrow through."

"And Tyrannus?"

"Tyrannus is insane. His mind is filled with madness. He is ever-changing. I am unchanging—"

"Like the rock you burrow through?" Theodore called out.

Everyone glared at him.

"Sorry." Theodore pretended to zip his lips shut.

"Will you help me, Charlie Benjamin?" Slagguron asked. "Your safety is guaranteed."

"How do I know you won't change your mind? That it will remain . . . unchanging, just like you say you are?"

"Look at my actions. I have already protected you once, from the Hydra."

Charlie glanced at the Mother Hydra. In all the chaos, he had actually forgotten about her. She hung back, clearly afraid of the colossal Named creature.

"Well, if we were on the debate squad," Charlie said, "someone—not me, of course—could argue that the only reason you saved me from her is because I couldn't help you if I was dead."

"So I saved you to *use* you?"

"Someone could argue that—not me, of course."

"But she is not threatening you now."

Charlie shrugged. "Not really. Not with you here."

"So I have nothing to gain from killing her now, do I?"

"I guess not."

Suddenly, Slagguron whipped his massive body forward and slammed himself down on the Mother Hydra with the force of a building collapsing. She was crushed instantly under his incredible weight. When he rose back up to his full height, her corpse—leaking black ichor—didn't even twitch.

"Why . . . why did you do that?" Charlie said, aghast. He was stunned by the Named Lord's sudden, unprovoked violence.

"It was just a token. A small gift from me to you."

A *gift*?

Charlie could barely speak. It wasn't as if he cared about the Mother Hydra—after all, she had just tried to eat him—but that was only after he had messed with her babies and stolen her milk. She had a right to be at least a little angry, didn't she?

But now she was dead.

Even worse, they had lost the opportunity to ever get her restorative milk again . . . or maybe that was Slagguron's plan all along.

"I . . . I don't know what to say."

"Help me now and I will protect you, Charlie

Benjamin. You have my word. My word, like me, is unchanging."

Charlie didn't know how to respond. It had clearly come to the point where he had to make a choice, but all of his options seemed terrible.

He could try to portal away with his friends, but after seeing the sheer speed of Slagguron, he knew they couldn't do it in time. The only other option was to do as Slagguron asked and bring him to Earth—but that was madness, wasn't it? After his failure with Barakkas there was no way Charlie was going to be responsible for bringing another Lord of the Nether into the world, even to save his own life.

But was that a choice he could make for his friends? If he had a chance to save them, even a slight one, shouldn't he take it?

"Let's just kill him!" Theodore shouted from across the cavern, his eyes filled with manic energy. "We got the DT on our side, not to mention Ms. Ax Attack. Plus I can sling a portal with the best of them, and then there's Pinch, who can do . . . well, whatever it is that Pinch does. Trust me, that big worm doesn't stand a chance!"

"Does your brain ever communicate with your mouth?" Violet asked incredulously.

"Hey, is it my fault I'm feeling confident? I'm just

tired of being bullied by these big bad boys. Let's do this thing! Let's kill this sucker!"

"No," Charlie said. The word echoed across the cavern with calm finality.

"What do you mean, *no*?" Theodore asked. "What else are we gonna do? I mean, you're definitely not gonna portal him to Earth, are you?"

"Actually," Charlie said, "that's exactly what I'm going to do."

"What?" Violet shouted.

"You can't be serious," Pinch added.

"I'm deadly serious."

Charlie closed his eyes. Brilliant purple fire raced across him, and he opened a portal just large enough for Slagguron to slither through. On the other side was Death Valley: a flat, featureless desert with only some cactus and a lone rattlesnake curled up under a rock to break the terrible monotony.

"There," he said to Slagguron. "I didn't know where you wanted to go, exactly, but the desert is pretty open. You should be able to get underground in no time."

Slagguron stared at the portal suspiciously. "I . . . did not expect you to do as I asked."

"Then why did you?"

"I have been following you for some time, Charlie Benjamin. Tracking you by the vibration of your footfalls—they are unique. Specific. I wanted to gain your trust."

"And now you have and I've done what you wanted, so go on through." Charlie gestured toward the open portal. "Earth awaits."

Slagguron stared at the fiery gateway but made no move to enter it.

"No," he said finally. "This is a trap. You mean to close it on me. Cut me in half, like you once did to Barakkas's arm."

"Look, you wanted my trust," Charlie said, "and I gave it to you. Now you won't trust me in return? Why don't you just kill me if you don't believe me? Kill all of us."

"Charlie!" Violet cried out, horrified.

"You are sly," Slagguron replied. "Deceitful, like Verminion."

"Only a liar believes everyone is lying to them."

"Are you calling me a liar?" Slagguron thundered, rising to his full height, his voice deepening with barely controlled rage. "I am unchanging—"

"Like the rock you burrow through. Yeah, yeah, I've heard you sing that song before." Charlie shook his head impatiently. "Look, you gonna go through the portal or you gonna kill me? Just pick one already. I'm getting bored."

Slagguron stared at Charlie with his large black eyes. Finally, he shook his great head. "We will meet again."

He leaped into the air like a swimmer off the high dive as hard, protective panels snapped across his face, creating a point like a drill bit. With amazing ease, he burrowed back into the ground, leaving behind a giant tunnel that snaked away into the dark recesses of the Nether.

Within moments, he was gone.

"Wow," Theodore said, his jaw hanging open in astonishment.

"I can't believe that just happened," Violet seconded.

Pinch, however, was focused on something else. The adult Hydras were closing in on them, mouths widening, teeth glistening with drool. "I think it might be wise for us to make a hasty exit."

"You may be right," Violet agreed, glancing around at the monsters as they prepared to avenge the death of their Queen.

Suddenly, one of the Hydras leaped out of the pool next to Charlie and lunged at him, snapping furiously. Instinctively, Charlie drew his rapier and lopped off two of the beast's heads. The instant he did, the giant portal to Death Valley slammed shut—a stark reminder that not even a Double-Threat could Nethermance and Banish at the same time.

"Theodore! Open a portal!" Charlie yelled, running to join the group as he fended off the remaining heads of the Hydra. "We need to get outa here, pronto!"

Theodore worked on making a portal as Charlie and Violet—back to back—frantically swung their weapons, creating a heap of Hydra heads.

"Duck!" Pinch shouted.

They did, narrowly avoiding a tail swipe from the nearest beast.

"Get ready," Theodore yelled. "Here it comes!"

His portal snapped open.

The four of them leaped through it, followed by another Hydra. Theodore quickly closed the portal behind them, slicing the pursuing creature in two, forcing it to suffer the same terrible fate that Slagguron had so recently feared for himself.

Several students crowded around Charlie, Pinch, Violet, and Theodore, checking out the slaughtered Hydra that lay on the warm sand of the beach in front of the Nightmare Academy.

"Take a good look!" Theodore said proudly. "That

critter just got NM'd—Nethermanced! That's a Theodore Dagget specialty."

He pronounced it *spesh-ee-al-it-ee*.

"Why did you do it?" Violet asked, pulling Charlie away from the group, while Theodore continued to regale the crowd with his accomplishments. "Why did you open that portal for Slagguron?"

"To kill him. I meant to close it on him, just like he said. I guess I wasn't clever enough."

"Indeed," Pinch said, walking up. "And what if you hadn't been *fast* enough, either, allowing him to escape to Earth, unharmed?"

"He didn't."

"He could have. That was quite a gamble, young man."

"Isn't everything? Besides, if I hadn't opened the portal, he would have killed us anyway. It put him on the defensive. I thought keeping him off balance was our best chance for survival."

"Well, it worked," Violet said. "I gotta give you credit for that, although I still don't know why Slagguron just left like he did."

"Because it was a stalemate," Charlie replied. "He didn't trust the portal I made but he also didn't want to kill me, because only the Headmaster and I can make a portal big enough for him to escape through and he wanted to keep that option open in the future."

"But why? Why would he ever trust another portal from you if he didn't trust this one?"

"Gosh, I don't know, Violet," Charlie replied with a sudden flash of anger. "Unfortunately, he forgot to invite me to his 'Escape from the Nether' planning party."

"Hey, relax! Don't be such a smart aleck. I'm trying to figure all this out just like you."

"Sorry," Charlie said, chagrined. "I guess I'm just frustrated because I know he's up to something but I don't know what."

"Maybe this was just plan A? Maybe he was just trying his luck with you, seeing if you'd panic and open a portal that he could escape through—but once he saw how tough you were, he knew he couldn't bully you, so he moved on to plan B."

"Which is?"

"I don't know," Violet said with a sigh. "Maybe plan B has nothing to do with you. Maybe he'll just try to escape through the Anomaly if the Guardian dies."

"But how would he get up to it?"

Violet pursed her lips, thinking. "Tyrannus? Do you think Tyrannus is strong enough to carry him there?"

Charlie shrugged. "Could be. But none of that will

matter, as long as the Guardian stays healthy, which reminds me"—he turned to Pinch—"do you have the milk?"

Pinch held up the Chapstick container. "Indeed I do."

"Excellent. We better get it to the Headmaster right away. It's supposed to restore anyone who drinks it to when they were most powerful. I sure hope that's true."

"So do I," Pinch said.

Then, to everyone's astonishment, he took the cap off the Chapstick container and, licking his lips, drank the milk of the Mother Hydra.

· CHAPTER TWELVE ·
PINCH THE POWERFUL

"What . . . what did you just do?" Charlie cried out, numb with shock.

"Simply what was necessary," Pinch replied. "We can't very well give something as important as this to the Guardian without testing it first, now, can we?"

"But you drank all of it!"

"Not all of it. Just one sip, in fact. There's another one left, see?" He showed them the tiny container. There was, in fact, a little bit of the Hydra milk left in it.

"You thief!" Charlie shouted. "The Mother Hydra is dead. If that's not enough to save the Guardian, we can't get any more!"

"Hey, guys," Theodore said cheerfully, walking over to them, oblivious of what had just happened. He was still basking in the glow of the attention from the other students over his Hydra kill. "You know, this Nethermancy thing isn't half bad. See, you just have to figure out how to use it for offense. I mean, it's true that you can't win without a good defense but, you know, everyone likes to score sometimes." He eyed Charlie and Violet curiously. "What's wrong? You guys look like you just saw an Acidspitter in your cornflakes."

"What's wrong," Violet said, "is that Pinch drank the Hydra milk."

"What?" Theodore cried out, turning to him. "Are you deranged?"

"Just a sip," Pinch replied.

"Just a—" Unable to contain his rage, Theodore stormed toward the man, rolling his sleeves up over his skinny arms as if readying for battle. "After all we went through just to get that stupid stuff, you decided to take some yourself? I don't care if you *are* an adult—I'm gonna knock your head clean off!"

"Wait!" Charlie yelled.

"What?"

"Look."

Something was happening to Pinch. His face was contorted in pain, and all his muscles were tensed as if he'd just been zapped with a cattle prod. He began to shake violently. Charlie, scared the man was going to spill the remaining milk, rushed over and took the container from him, capping it immediately.

"What's wrong?" Violet asked.

"I . . . I don't know . . . ," the bearded man groaned. He dropped to his knees, closed his eyes tightly, and cried out in agony. "Oh, it hurts!"

"Something's gone wrong," Charlie said. "Somebody get somebody! Get Mama Rose!"

But before anyone could move, a curious thing happened—

All the hair in Pinch's beard fell out of his face and dropped to the sand below. It was a shocking sight—he looked so different now that he was clean shaven, so much younger.

And that's when Charlie realized that it wasn't just the lack of beard that was making him look younger. He actually *was* younger. The wrinkles around his mouth and eyes had smoothed out, the few extra pounds he carried around his middle had melted away, and he had begun to shrink, losing one inch off his height, then two, then more.

"What's happening?" Violet whispered.

Charlie shook his head. "I really don't know."

The wrinkles, inches, and pounds continued to fall off Pinch until his gray suit hung on him so loosely that he looked like a child playing dress-up in Daddy's clothes. The skin of his face was unblemished, and the whites of his eyes were clear and strong.

"Absolutely incredible," Pinch said, and Charlie was shocked to hear that he now sounded like a teenager. "It worked! The elixir actually worked—it returned me to when I was most powerful!"

Charlie stared in awe at the thirteen-year-old boy who stood in front of him: the thirteen-year-old boy who used to be Pinch.

He had become a kid again.

"NP," Theodore muttered in disbelief. "Not possible."

Violet shook her head. "I don't believe it."

"I wonder," Pinch said in that strange, prepubescent voice of his, "if the Gift has returned, along with my youth."

He held out his right hand and closed his eyes. Purple fire crackled across him, and in the long shadow of the Nightmare Academy, a large portal snapped open, leading to the darkness of the Nether.

They all looked through it, astonished.

"You did it," Theodore exclaimed. "You actually opened a portal!"

"You got the Gift back," Charlie said. "You really did!"

"I did, didn't I?" Pinch replied, and then began to weep with happiness.

That's truly bizarre, Charlie thought, as he watched Pinch wearing the jeans and red t-shirt he'd just loaned him. They fit well. The boy (*man,* Charlie reminded himself) was about his size and weight, but that's where the similarities ended—Pinch's hair was dark, as were his eyes, and his complexion was as pale as a flounder's belly.

"Here it is," Pinch said, pulling a weathered case out from under the hammock where he slept. His cabin in the Nightmare Academy was small and spare—there were no pictures, no personal effects, no comforts of home. He brushed the dust off the case, then opened it with something like reverence.

Inside lay a shiny weapon with a sharp, curved blade and a beautifully detailed handle made of onyx.

"My sickle," Pinch said with an almost gleeful grin, lifting it. The moment his hand touched it, the weapon glowed with a cold blue fire. "I haven't picked this up since . . ." He let his voice trail off. "Well, since a long time ago."

"Pinch," Charlie prodded gently.

"Yes?"

"We need to leave. The Headmaster is waiting for the milk."

"Indeed." Pinch stood, still gripping the sickle.

"Do *you* want to portal us there," Charlie asked, "or—"

"You do it. I'm a bit out of practice."

"Okay." Charlie turned to Violet and Theodore. "Get ready. We're going to be heading straight into the 5th Ring, as close to the BT Graveyard as I can get us. There's gonna be monsters there—maybe a ton."

"Do you have the milk?" Violet asked.

Charlie nodded. "Sure do." He checked his pocket anyway. The elixir was there, safe and sound. "Okay, here we go." Purple flames crackled across him as he began to open a portal.

The 5th Ring was crawling with monsters. Charlie was dismayed to see that the vicious beasts had gotten much closer to where the Guardian was holed up— some of them had managed to get near enough to touch the ruined ships on the outskirts of the BT Graveyard.

"Oh, dear," Pinch said. "They've advanced significantly. The Guardian must be very weak. His aura is waning. I hope we're not too late."

"We have to hurry." Charlie drew his rapier. "I wish I had a great plan to tell you—something smart and clever—but it looks like we're just gonna have to fight our way to the graveyard."

"That's pretty far," Violet said, eyeing the many monster-filled yards they would have to travel.

"True, but we've got one more Banisher with us now."

"Indeed you do." Pinch raised his curved sickle. It glowed with a blue brilliance, clearly a far finer weapon than the ones Charlie and Violet carried.

"Theodore?" Charlie said.

"That's my name, don't wear it out."

"You just be ready to portal us out in case things go bad, okay?"

"Yeah, sure. I guess that's all I'm good for since I'm not a Banisher like the rest of you."

Normally, Charlie would have tried to lift his pal's spirits, but there was just no time. In the scant few seconds that the portal had been open, the power of the Guardian had diminished even further, and the monsters of the Nether were beginning to make their way into the heart of the BT Graveyard.

"Here we go," Charlie said. Rapier raised high, he rushed through the portal and into the Nether, followed by the others.

It wasn't long before the first attack.

Two Class-5 Dangeroos plummeted out of the sky to land in front of them with a thud. The monsters bared their fangs and growled, acting nothing like the friendly animals that they vaguely resembled. Wasting no time, Charlie, Violet, and Pinch waded in, weapons flying.

He's good, Charlie thought as he watched Pinch wield his sickle. Even though it had been years since Pinch had used his powers, the weapon flashed and twisted expertly under his command.

"First one's down!" Violet yelled, and then they all turned their attention to the second Dangeroo. Deadly as the creature was, the three skilled Banishers cut it down to size in a matter of moments.

And that was when they heard the small voice from behind them:

"Help me . . ."

Charlie turned to see a little boy about seven years old standing with his back to the tangled, mustard-colored crystals of the 5th Ring. He was crying, his eyes wild with panic.

"They took me!" the child screamed. "Those kangaroo monsters—I had a nightmare!"

"They must have snatched him and sent him to finish off the Guardian," Violet said. "What do you want to do?"

Charlie glanced around quickly. Now alerted to their presence, Class-5 monsters were closing in on them from all sides. Charlie could even see some of them creeping up behind the boy through the razor-sharp crystals.

"We gotta get that kid outa here. Right now. Back to the Academy."

"No time," Pinch shot back. "We must get the milk to the Guardian first. That is absolutely vital."

"I agree, but if we take the kid with us, he'll slow us down."

"We can't just leave him here!" Violet said. "He'll die!"

"Everyone will die if the Guardian dies!" Pinch replied.

Charlie closed his eyes in thought. The Headmaster had warned him that there might be other kids stranded in the Nether and that he should save them if he could, but she'd also said that nothing was more important than fulfilling their mission and getting the milk to the Guardian as soon as possible. It was a tough choice.

"All right," he said finally. "We'll split up. Theodore,

you go portal the kid back to the Academy. Violet, you go with him and protect him while he does."

"But what about the milk?" Theodore asked.

"Pinch and I will get it to the Guardian."

"I don't know," Violet said. "I'm not sure if it's a good idea for us to separate like that."

"They're coming!" the little boy screamed as he spotted the monsters approaching from behind: A couple of Netherstalkers and what looked like a Darkling were slithering toward the child through the gloom.

"Go now!" Charlie yelled. "We're out of time!"

Still a little unsure, Theodore and Violet ran back toward the frightened boy as Pinch responded to an incoming attack by a Netherbat with a furious flurry of strokes from his sickle. Charlie joined in and soon they were engaged in desperate combat with several of the flying Nethercreatures.

Theodore, meanwhile, was focusing on opening a portal back to the Nightmare Academy while Violet's ax rose and fell against the Darkling and Netherstalkers that threatened to eat the little boy.

"How's that portal?" she shouted as the petrified child wrapped his arms around her waist, weeping heavily.

"Here it comes!"

Theodore's portal popped open right in front of them. Through it, they could see the sandy beach in front of the Nightmare Academy.

"Perfect!" Violet said. "Follow me!" She and the little boy rushed into the portal, followed by Theodore.

As soon as they were on the other side, Theodore turned back to Charlie. "We made it!" he shouted. "Everything's cool here!"

"Great!" Charlie yelled as he and Pinch killed the last of the attacking Netherbats. "Now close the portal before anything else gets through!"

"Wait!" Violet shouted, eyes wide. She began to back away from the child they had just rescued. "Uh, Charlie? You better take a look at this."

Charlie turned and, looking through the portal, saw the little boy standing on the beach, shaking violently. At first, he thought that the kid was just so scared that he couldn't stop trembling, but then Charlie noticed something odd—

The boy's face began to droop and then it actually *melted*, running off his skull like hot candle wax.

"Do you remember what I said about being as unchanging as the rock I burrow through?" the boy cackled with a crazy, distorted grin. "I lied."

Oh no, Charlie thought. *It* can't *be.*

The rest of the child's skin slid away to reveal a wormlike creature underneath. Around its middle was a blackly glittering Artifact of the Nether.

"Slagguron," Charlie gasped.

"Told you we'd meet again," the Third Named replied with a laugh.

· CHAPTER THIRTEEN ·
SLAGGURON THE CHANGELING

"He's a Changeling!" Violet exclaimed as Slagguron started growing. Soon, he was nearly half the size of the Nightmare Academy itself.

"What's a Changeling?" Theodore asked, backing away from the morphing creature.

"They're like Mimics, but instead of turning into a copy of something, they can turn into anything they want—but only for short periods of time."

"All very true," Slagguron boomed. "You thought you had outsmarted me in the Hydra cave, but who is the smart one now? As soon as you said you were planning to rescue stranded children, I knew your pathetic human desire to 'do good' would lead to my victory!"

"And he accused *me* of being sly," Charlie muttered,

as he and Pinch watched Slagguron's transformation from their vantage point in the Nether.

"Well, he certainly fooled us," Pinch said darkly. "I had no idea that this was his true nature. We thought no one had ever laid eyes on Slagguron, but who knows how many times we saw him and just didn't know it?"

"Charlie, what do we do?" Violet yelled through the portal, but before he could answer, it snapped closed, leaving Violet and Theodore at the Nightmare Academy while Charlie and Pinch remained in the Nether.

"Should we go back and help them?" Pinch asked.

Charlie shook his head. "No. To help them, we have to go forward."

He turned to see a flood of monsters coming toward them now that the distraction of Slagguron was gone.

"You ready to do this, Pinch?"

"Oh, I'm ready," Pinch replied. "Are you?"

"Definitely."

Charlie rushed toward the attacking Class 5s, weapon raised. Pinch followed, only steps behind. They closed the distance between themselves and the BT Graveyard in a blur of swinging steel, sticky black ichor, and flying monster parts. As they fought, Charlie glanced over at Pinch and was shocked to see how elegantly the boy (*man*, he stubbornly corrected himself) banished his share of Nethercreatures. He was awesomely good, and Charlie was struck once again by what a crime it was that the Nightmare Division had tried to destroy such an astonishing talent.

Soon, almost without realizing it, Charlie and Pinch found themselves safe in the BT Graveyard, leaving behind a trail of dead, bleeding monsters.

"Quite remarkable," Pinch said, glancing back at their handiwork. "We did all that?"

Charlie nodded. "Not bad for a thirteen-year-old and a guy who *looks* like a thirteen-year-old."

Pinch laughed, and for just a moment Charlie could see the boy he must once have been—the boy who had only wanted to do good and be liked.

But then Pinch grew serious again. "Where's the Guardian?"

"This way," Charlie replied. Running through the maze of wrecked ships, he led Pinch toward the one where the Guardian made its home.

I wonder what's going on back at the Nightmare Academy, Charlie thought with dread, weaving through the towering hulks of boats that would never again see an ocean. *Has Slagguron started his attack? Are my friends even still alive?*

The students of the Nightmare Academy rushed out onto all the available decks, catwalks, and branches, staring in silent awe at the Lord of the Nether. Brooke watched from the pirate ship at the very top with Geoff by her side.

"Wow," she said. "I can promise you one thing: This wouldn't have happened if I'd gone with them."

"Riiiight," Geoff replied skeptically.

"The Guardian is dead," Slagguron roared. "Or close to it. The crippling effects of its aura are now no more than a tickle. I have waited many long years to come to Earth and start my destruction."

"Well, you know what they say?" Theodore yelled up to him, still standing on the beach. "The bigger they are, the harder they fall!"

"They also say something else," Slagguron thundered in reply. "Might makes right—which makes me very, *very* right."

"Hey, you!" a voice shouted in a thick southern twang.

Slagguron swiveled his head to see Mama Rose standing on the deck of the Academy's galley. Food for lunch was laid out carefully on worn, wooden tables.

"That's right, I'm talking to you, fella! Now, I know you're a big dang deal and all, but these are just kids around here—kids who should be inside and not out gawking at the giant monster!" She directed that last part at the students behind her. They scattered, disappearing into the ships of the Academy like frightened mice. She turned back to Slagguron. "Now, I know you wanna do some killin', but you gotta take it somewhere else. I'm sure even a big ol' Lord of the Nether like you don't wanna be hurtin' children!"

"That," Slagguron said, "is where you're wrong."

Then, with the force of a thousand wrecking balls, he reared back and slammed his body into the trunk of the banyan tree.

Charlie was pretty sure he had never seen anything as close to death as the Guardian. The frail creature was now a sickly yellow. Its chest rose and fell in shallow, wheezing gasps. Its big eyes were glassy and unfocused, and its cracked skin wept a thin, puslike fluid.

"Oh no," Charlie said. "Are we too late?"

"It's still breathing," Pinch replied.

Just then, the Headmaster entered behind Charlie and Pinch. "I'm sorry I wasn't here when you first arrived," she said. "I had to banish some Acidspitters that had drawn too close."

With a quick snap of her wrist, she collapsed her metal staff, now black with monster blood, to the size of a small rod and put it away in a fold of her dress.

"Who is this?" she said, glancing at Pinch.

"It's me, Edward," he replied. "Edward *Pinch*."

The Headmaster's eyes widened. "I see. I *see*. . . . This must mean that you got the milk, then?"

Charlie nodded. "Here you go."

He handed the Chapstick tube to the Headmaster.

She took it from him gratefully, breathing a sigh of relief. "Thank you very much, Mr. Benjamin . . . and Mr. Pinch. I'm sure you both have many interesting adventures to speak of, and I would like to hear them all—as soon as the Guardian has recovered, of course. As you can see, he is feeling poorly."

"Please, give it to him," Charlie said. "We need him strong. Right away."

The Headmaster held Charlie's gaze. "Why do I have the feeling that you have something . . . unfortunate to tell me, Mr. Benjamin?"

"I do. And I will. After you give the Guardian the milk."

Suddenly, a horrible shriek ripped through the Nether. It was so close that the glass windows of the warship shattered from the vibration.

"Tyrannus draws near," the Headmaster said. "He knows the Guardian will soon be dead."

She removed the cap from the tube and, careful not to touch the creature, poured the last of the elixir into the dying Guardian's mouth.

The impact was astonishing.

The sheer force of Slagguron's assault caused the great tree to rock violently. Two boats—a clipper ship where Mama Rose stood that served as the Academy's galley and a small sloop that was home to the laundry—were ripped from the branches on which they rested. The people inside screamed as they plunged to the ground.

Theodore, acting purely on instinct, lashed out with his right hand, instantly creating a large portal beneath the falling vessels. They sailed through it and into the 1st Ring of the Nether—a hundred feet in the air.

Without thinking, Theodore leaped into the portal after them.

As he fell through the Nether alongside the spiraling ships, he closed the portal above him and then opened a new one below, causing the boats to plummet through that portal and straight into the ocean in front of the Nightmare Academy, where they landed in a great explosion of water. The impact was rough, but not nearly as devastating as it would have been if the ships had slammed into solid ground.

After plunging into the warm ocean himself, Theodore surfaced and started to help the injured people escape from the sinking vessels. The first one he came to was Mama Rose.

"Well, look at you, boy," she said with a smile as Theodore pulled her free. "You may just have a future at this Nethermancy thing after all."

"Imagine that," Theodore said, smiling back.

As he continued to rescue the victims of Slagguron's first attack, Violet—blind with rage—raced toward the Named beast, ax at the ready. She grabbed on to the lowest of his centipedelike legs and, using them as a ladder, began to climb up them toward his massive head.

"What do you think you're doing?" Slagguron said, noticing her the way a horse might notice a fly. With one quick shake of his body, he sent Violet soaring. She tumbled wildly through the air, toward the Nightmare Academy, and slammed hard into the rough-hewn railing of the pirate ship. She tried to grab on to it but missed and started to tumble to the ground far below, when she heard a familiar voice—

"Got you!"

Brooke snatched Violet by the arm. With one strong yank, she pulled the young Banisher up onto the deck of the ship.

"Thanks," Violet said, out of breath. "If you hadn't been here . . ."

"Don't mention it." Brooke smiled warmly.

Violet turned and jumped onto one of the Nightmare Academy's elevatorlike dinghies. She swung it back and forth on its long rope like a pendulum. Then, using all her strength, she leaped from the dinghy and onto Slagguron's buglike face, where his thousands of short, waving arms couldn't reach.

"Get off me, human!" he roared.

Without a word, Violet raised her ax and sank it deep into the great beast's left eye.

He screamed in pain so loudly that the ground trembled.

"Now, you die!" he thundered, then reared back to slam Violet into the Academy's massive trunk.

"No!" Theodore yelled. *"Violet!"*

But just before Slagguron could smear Violet against the side of the great tree, the Named beast screamed in agony and collapsed to the ground with the force of an asteroid hitting the Earth. Violet rode him all the way down, using the meat of his body to cushion the enormous impact of the fall.

"Unbelievable!" Theodore said, racing up to her. "Did you do that to him?"

Violet shook her head. "No way."

Slagguron tried to rise before collapsing, once again, to the ground.

"What's wrong with him?" Theodore asked.

"Charlie and Pinch must have revived the Guardian!" Violet exclaimed happily. She slid down the side of the huge creature and landed on the sand with cat-like agility. "The Academy's defenses are back up."

"Wow, look how strong the Guardian's aura is! Even all the way out here, it's still totally crippling."

Hard plates slammed down over Slagguron's face, creating a point like a drill bit. Violet realized that she had seen him do this once before. "He's getting ready to escape!" she shouted.

"Uh-oh, I think you're right."

Without another word, Theodore opened a portal to the 1st Ring of the Nether.

"What in the world are you doing?"

"You'll see," he said, and ran through.

The Guardian's recovery was astonishing.

Moments after he drank the Hydra milk, the sickly orange color of his skin faded, replaced by a green that looked vibrant and healthy. His cloudy eyes became clear, and even though he was not a large creature, his body seemed to fill out and strengthen.

"All right!" Charlie exclaimed. "He's getting better!"

Then, from all around them, they heard screams of pain.

Charlie ran out on the deck to see the many beasts of the Nether retreating in agony as the aura of the Guardian flowed out across the graveyard of ships. The loudest shriek of all came from above, as Tyrannus tumbled violently out of the sky to crash into the harsh ground in an explosion of mustard-colored crystals.

"TREACHERY!" he screamed, staggering to his feet, his bat wings twisted comically beneath him. "Unfair! Unfair! The Guardian should be DEAD so I can paint the ground RED with blood from your HEAD!"

"Actually," Charlie said, turning to Pinch, "Theodore came up with the last part of that rhyme."

The Headmaster walked out to join them. "As you can see, the Guardian is strong once again. Come, we must now return to the Nightmare Academy."

"If it's still there," Charlie muttered.

"What was that, Mr. Benjamin?"

"I said I can't wait to get there."

She walked past them, away from the portal-dampening effect of the great, red Anomaly up above. Charlie turned to follow until he heard a small, soft voice behind him.

"Hold me," the Guardian said, standing in the

doorway of the ship it called home. "It's so cold here in the Nether, and so lonely. . . ."

He's right. It is lonely in the Nether, Charlie thought, staring into the pleading eyes of the gentle creature. *What a sad, miserable life it leads—he can't touch anything here, and no humans can touch* him.

"Sorry, Hank," Charlie said softly. "You know I can't do that. I have to go now. Good luck to you."

Tearing his eyes away from the frail, needy creature, Charlie turned and ran after the Headmaster. After all this time in the Nether, he was desperate to get back to his friends.

As Charlie and Pinch arrived at the Nightmare Academy through a portal made by the Headmaster, Slagguron, still in terrible pain, rose up into the air. With all his remaining strength, he dived headfirst into the ground. There was a great explosion of sand and soon he was gone from view, leaving behind an enormous tunnel that snaked into the dark depths of the Earth.

"Slagguron," the Headmaster said.

Charlie glanced nervously at her. "That's what I wanted to tell you about, actually. He, um . . . well, he escaped from the Nether."

"I would say he did."

"It's a long story."

"I would expect it is."

"Well, that's that," Pinch said, running a hand wearily across his boyish face. Charlie still couldn't get used to the fact that he now looked like a thirteen-year-old. "We've lost him."

"No, actually, we haven't."

They turned to see Theodore standing next to his still-open portal.

"What do you mean, Mr. Dagget?" the Headmaster asked, walking over.

"Well, just before Slagguron left, when he was lying there all crippled, I opened this portal."

Charlie looked through it and was surprised to see a familiar sight: his equipment closet on the 1st ring of the Nether. "Hey, that's where I keep all my Banishing gear!"

Theodore nodded. "I remembered. You had the battery in there for attracting Gremlins, and some spare rapiers, and I also noticed that you had a handful of interesting little things on the top shelf."

He held up a small, metal object.

"A tracking device," Charlie said.

"Yup. I attached one of them to Slagguron's belt just before he left." Theodore smiled so widely that Charlie was afraid his head would split in two. "Go on, tell me I'm a supergenius."

"You, sir, are a super-*duper* genius."

"Yes, that's quite clever," the Headmaster agreed. "I commend you on your quick thinking, Mr. Dagget. As always, we are now facing a mixture of good and bad. Slagguron has escaped to Earth, which is quite clearly bad; but he will now possibly lead us to the new lair of Barakkas and Verminion, which is potentially quite good. Also, as a result of your extraordinary efforts to get the Hydra milk to save the Guardian, Tyrannus remains stranded in the Nether—again, very good. All in all, well done."

Charlie, Theodore, and Violet beamed.

"So what now?" Pinch asked. "What's our next step?"

"Tyrannus may be in the Nether for the moment," the Headmaster replied, "but there is no way to guarantee that he won't find another means of crossing over to Earth sometime in the future. If that happens, the Four Named will most certainly summon the Fifth, which is something that we absolutely cannot allow. Our path is quite clear. It's all or nothing now—we must fight to the last man."

She turned to face the ocean, her dress blowing in the warm breeze.

"One of the Named must die."

PART
· III ·
The Named

· CHAPTER FOURTEEN ·
PLAN OF ATTACK

The sails on the pirate ship at the very top of the Nightmare Academy snapped in the breeze, distracting Violet. She was concentrating furiously, trying to draw a dragon while workmen from the Division did their best to repair the massive damage from Slagguron.

The drawing wasn't going well.

She used to be able to see the images in her mind as clearly as a photograph, which made the act of sketching a simple question of transferring them to paper. But the pictures weren't coming to her clearly now, as if she were seeing them through a milky haze.

"How's it going?" Brooke asked, walking up to her.

"It's going," Violet said, unhappy with the interruption.

"I just wanted to say you were amazing before—

attacking Slagguron like that. It was like watching a seriously experienced Banisher. Better, actually. I've never seen anyone do anything like that."

"Thanks. And thanks for grabbing me like you did. I wouldn't have made it without you."

Brooke shrugged. "Right place, right time, that's all." She flipped her silken hair away from her eyes.

"Well, thanks again." Violet went back to concentrating on her drawing, praying that Brooke would get the message and move on.

She didn't.

"Why do you hate me so much?" Brooke asked finally.

Violet looked up at her. "What?"

"Look, I get that I'm not the most wonderful person in the world—in fact, I know I can be annoying at times."

"Just annoying?"

"Okay, seriously annoying. Probably even worse than that. And I know we got off on the wrong foot when I first met you guys here at the Academy."

"You *think*?"

Brooke and Geoff's constant attacks on Charlie and the rest of them were still fresh in Violet's mind, even though they had happened over six long months ago.

"I'm just saying," Brooke continued, "—geez, you

really make this hard—I'm just saying that I know I was a pain before but I've tried my best to change. I've worked hard at being nice to you. I just want to be your friend."

"Why?"

Brooke seemed genuinely surprised by the question. "Well . . . I don't know. For the reason anyone wants to be someone's friend, I guess."

"Yes, but why?"

"Because I like you and I thought we might get along."

Violet shook her head. "That's not it. The reason is that you want to be near Charlie Benjamin."

"You're crazy—he's thirteen and I'm nearly sixteen!"

"He's also a Double-Threat: the most powerful kid here. Everyone knows it. You just want to be close to him, and you want to be friends with me because I'm friends with Charlie."

Violet went back to her sketch. It was truly looking terrible.

"That's so mean," Brooke said, her eyes starting to fill with tears.

"And you can save the tears. As well as the little blond hair flip and the fake pouting. None of that stuff works on me."

"It's not fake!" Brooke snapped back. Violet could

feel the older girl's eyes on her but resisted the urge to meet them. "Never mind." Brooke turned to go . . . but instead of walking off, she just stopped and stood there. "I used to be able to portal," she said finally. "I was pretty good at it, too—but I lost the Gift and now all I can do is watch everyone around me use theirs and try to find some way to be a part of that."

"You got the Gift back, remember?" Violet looked up at her. "When you and Charlie were facing off with Barakkas in his lair? You opened a portal and saved both of you."

"But it didn't last. It went away again."

"Because you let it!" She jumped to her feet, truly angry now. "You could be like the rest of us if you tried, Brooke, but that takes guts. You'd rather be the pretty girlfriend—next to the power but not responsible for it!"

Violet was beginning to shake with rage. Brooke took a step back.

"Okay, maybe that's true, but that doesn't mean I want it to be."

"Then change it!"

"How? I just want to be like you."

Violet laughed. "No, you don't. Trust me."

"I *do*. You're tough and you're incredibly skillful and—"

"And I hate myself for it!"

To her horror, Violet realized that it was true: She did hate herself, or at least what she was becoming.

"I used to like to draw," she continued softly. "Now . . . look at this." She gestured at her stilted sketch in disgust. "When the monsters come and it's time to fight, I feel in control. I can swing my ax—I'm good at it, really good—but I don't recognize myself when I do it."

She was silent a moment, staring at the distant ocean. "I can feel myself slipping away. I'm just not sure who I am anymore."

"I am a seriously astonishing Nethermancer," Theodore said as he and Charlie walked along the beach in front of the Nightmare Academy, picking up shells. "You wouldn't believe these portals I opened before: huge! Big enough for two ships to fall through. Both of them dropped into the Nether—*boom!*—then I dived in after them and—while I was falling, mind you—I opened another giant portal, and they fell through that one just like threading a needle, and—*whoosh!*—they ended up right back here on Earth, right out there in the water, safe and sound."

He pointed to the spot in the ocean where the boats had hit.

"That's so awesome!" Charlie said, truly happy for his friend. "You used the portals to do something totally unexpected. It's like the super extreme version of what you and I did to bring sun to the Darkling, except you did it all by yourself. You must be totally thrilled!"

"Definitely."

Theodore suddenly stopped walking and bent over with a moan, clutching his stomach in what seemed like pain.

"What's wrong?" Charlie asked. "You're not getting sick, are you?"

Theodore shook his head, then looked up at his friend with fresh torment in his eyes. "The problem is I don't know how I did it. The portals, I mean—they just happened."

"So what?"

"So, if you asked me to do it again—right here, right now—there'd be no way. I can't repeat it. I'm a one-shot wonder! My career is over and I'm only thirteen!"

"Relax. That's the way it is for me, too. The big stuff, the giant portals, those just happen. They come from somewhere deep inside and I can't control them. That's what makes them so powerful . . . and so dangerous."

"Really?" Theodore seemed almost hopeful.

Charlie nodded. "Look, you did something great today and, when the moment comes again, and I know it will, I'm sure you'll do something even better."

"You think?"

"Absolutely! And just imagine how your dad's gonna feel when he hears about this."

Theodore's eyes lit up. "You think someone will tell him?"

"Are you kidding? Someone? How about everyone!"

Theodore was suddenly filled with happiness. "He's really gonna be proud, isn't he? He pretty much can't help but be, right?"

"Definitely."

"I mean, he was already kind of heading in that direction. Remember, back in Barakkas and Verminion's lair, when my dad said it was good how I refused to leave so I could be there to protect you?"

Charlie nodded.

"Well, this is that times ten, right? I protected a lot of people today!"

"You sure did." Charlie clapped his friend on the shoulder. "Trust me, this is a turning point."

"A turning point . . ."

Charlie could almost see Theodore thinking it through, imagining all the wonderful new possibilities in his relationship with his father.

"You're a good friend, you know that, Charlie?" he said finally. "The best I ever had. Truly."

"Stop it." Charlie waved Theodore's words away, embarrassed.

"Don't do that! I mean it. I won't ever let anything happen to you. I swear."

"Okay." Charlie was impressed by his friend's seriousness. "Same here."

They stared out at the ocean. Gulls dived from the sky and plunged into the water, filling their bills with tasty fish.

"When was the last time you saw your folks?" Theodore asked after a while, breaking the quiet.

Charlie shrugged. "Long time. Six months. I don't even know where they are."

"The Division still has them under wraps for their own protection?"

Charlie nodded. "I miss them."

I miss them.

The truth of those three simple words made his heart ache.

"Hey," Theodore said, eyes twinkling mischievously. "Wanna find out where they are? We could hack into the Division's computers, then make a stealth run and go see them."

"Nah."

"Could be fun," Theodore taunted. "Doing sneaky things, not following the rules, getting into trouble . . . just like old times."

"I appreciate it. Truly. But Verminion almost killed my parents before because of me. And now, with *three* of the Named on Earth, who knows what kind of danger they'll be in if I go see them?" Charlie shook his head. "It's best I'm not around them, trust me."

Just then, a portal snapped open in front of the two boys, and the Headmaster stepped through. "Mr. Benjamin, you have been summoned to the Nightmare Division. Something big is happening—get going."

She turned to leave.

"Wait a minute!" Charlie called out. "Aren't you going, too?"

She shook her head. "I'm afraid that's not possible. I must return to the Nether and keep an eye on the Guardian."

"But he's healthy."

"For the moment, yes, but it will only take another touch from a human to put us right back to where we started, and you can be sure that Tyrannus will do all he can to make that happen."

Charlie figured that was true, but the Headmaster couldn't just live in the Nether, keeping an eye on the Guardian for the rest of her life, could she?

"When will you be back?" he asked.

"When it's *safe*," the Headmaster replied in a tone that suggested the issue was not up for further discussion. "Now get going, Mr. Benjamin."

"Not without me."

The Headmaster turned to Theodore. "You said something, Mr. Dagget?"

Theodore nodded. "If he goes, I go."

"That's quite a strong position to take."

"I'm quite a strong Nethermancer."

To Charlie's shock, the Headmaster actually smiled. "So I've heard. Go with him, then. In fact, Mr. Benjamin, you may as well bring all your friends—you can never have too many, you know."

She walked off then, leaving Charlie and a stunned Theodore behind her.

"Going to the Nightmare Division, baby!" Theodore suddenly shouted. "That's the way *I* roll!"

It was cold and quiet in the High Council Chamber of the Nightmare Division. Scrubbed air whispered through vents. Computers hummed with soft clicks and chirps.

"We have found the new lair of Barakkas, Verminion, and Slagguron high in the frozen wastes of the Himalayas," Director Drake said to the assembled

Banishers and Nethermancers. "And yes, I included Slagguron in that group." He fixed Charlie with a withering stare. "It seems that our young friends at the Nightmare Academy saw fit to portal him to Earth."

The adults in the room grumbled but seemed unsurprised.

He just had to stick it to me, Charlie thought. Everyone knew about Slagguron escaping from the Nether— you couldn't keep news like that a secret—but leave it to the Director to make sure everyone knew who was responsible without explaining the circumstances. They thought they were saving a child, for crying out loud! A little kid! How were they supposed to know that Slagguron was a Changeling? No one else did.

"Yeah, they sure enough did do that," a voice said from the back of the room. Charlie recognized the Texas twang immediately. He turned to see Rex walk up the center aisle, and just the sight of the tall cowboy filled him with happiness. "But, near as I can tell, if they hadn't of portaled old Slagguron through, we wouldn't have found their new lair. That comes thanks to the smart thinkin' of Mister Theodore Dagget over there."

Rex nodded to Theodore, who blushed furiously and looked over at his father. The General glanced at his son, then shot him a quick wink.

"Hey! Did you see—"

"Yeah." Charlie smiled. "I sure did."

Rex fixed the Director with a stare. "Young Mr. Dagget was more clever than all the rest of us put together. We've been tryin' to find the new lair of the Named somethin' fierce, but we weren't even close—just running around like a buncha Hydras with our heads cut off."

He turned to Violet.

"Speaking of Hydra heads, how many of them you figure you cut off, while you were out there saving the Guardian, little Miss Violet Sweet?"

Violet, who sat on the other side of Charlie, turned beet red and shrugged. "No idea."

"I know, I know, they got six heads apiece, so it's mighty easy to lose count. I would have. That's the kinda thing a good Facilitator does for ya—and you had a pretty fine one in Miss Brooke Brighton, I gather, seeing as how she led you to the Guardian boat and got you into the BT Graveyard to begin with."

Brooke, who sat next to Violet, struggled to keep from breaking into the world's largest grin.

"But I'm sure you're right, Director," Rex continued, turning back to the man. "I guess those kids over there at the Academy are just a bunch of incompetent little morons."

The silence was thick and palpable.

"Thank you for your lovely speech, Banisher Henderson," Director Drake finally replied, voice heavy with sarcasm. "Did the children accomplish more than other children their own age? Unquestionably. But have they also caused more harm than other children? Absolutely."

He walked around his desk to stand directly in front of the crowd.

"Because of the actions of these youngsters, three of the four Named are now in our world. If Tyrannus finds his way here, the Four of them will summon the Fifth—but that won't happen. Now that we know the location of their new lair, we can finish what we started earlier. Ladies and gentlemen, we must complete the Division Invasion and kill one of the Named."

"Then let's make it Verminion," a high-pitched voice said from the side of the room. Charlie turned to see a boy walking toward the Director. He recognized him immediately.

It was Pinch.

"After all," Pinch continued, "Verminion was the one most gravely wounded during his fight with Barakkas. Consequently, he will be the most vulnerable. He should be first on our list to destroy."

"Thanks for the newsflash, squirt," Rex said, arms

crossed. "We'll definitely take that under advisement, but I hope you won't mind if we leave things open just a touch, in case we need to improvise."

"Improvise all you like," Pinch said, "as long as Verminion dies."

Rex stared at him. "Who the heck *are* you, kid?"

"You don't recognize me?"

"There's something familiar about you, but . . ." Rex walked closer, inspecting him. Suddenly, awareness filled the cowboy's eyes. "No . . . it can't be."

"I'm afraid it is."

"Pinch?" Rex asked cautiously.

"*Edward* Pinch, if you don't mind."

"What's going on here?" Director Drake asked.

"I'm wondering the same dang thing."

Charlie stood up. "I think I can explain. Pinch—I mean, Edward—drank some of the Hydra milk that we used to save the Guardian."

"I was testing it, you understand," Pinch explained. "We couldn't very well expose the creature to an unknown elixir without knowing if it was safe, could we?"

Charlie thought about calling Pinch on his heavy-handed twisting of the truth. After all, the boy *(man!)* had clearly been much more interested in regaining his former glory than in keeping the Guardian safe, but Charlie let it slide.

"Basically," Charlie continued, "the elixir returned Pinch—Edward, I mean—to when he was most powerful. Back to when he was a Double-Threat."

"It's not possible," Director Drake said, shaking his head. "Do you actually mean that this boy—man, I suppose—has regained the use of the Gift even after my predecessor at the Division ordered it surgically removed for the safety and security of all mankind?"

"Yes," Pinch replied dryly. "My Gift has returned. Perhaps you would like to try to have me Reduced once again—for the safety and security of all mankind, of course?"

"I would like that very much. It is bad enough that we have two Double-Threats running around, causing all manner of chaos. The thought of a third is positively mind-boggling. Reduction is a necessity!"

"That's not going to happen." Charlie walked up to stand next to Pinch. "I won't let it."

"See how they all stick together? They think they're a race unto themselves, don't they? No law applies to them. After all, they're Double-Threats: better, stronger, smarter than the rest of us!"

"That's not true!" Charlie turned to appeal to the people around him. "Look, I know I've done things that everyone wishes I hadn't—I wish the same thing—but none of it was done out of meanness or ego—"

"We know that," Drake interrupted. "And it doesn't matter. No one is accusing you of intentionally doing these terrible things you do. You didn't mean to bring Barakkas to our world and you surely didn't mean to bring Slagguron, either. But the fact is, you did. You *did*, Mr. Benjamin. And now the rest of us must clean up your unholy mess."

Charlie was desperate to reply. *I tried to help people,* he wanted to scream. *My parents, my friends, a lost kid in the Nether—how could that be wrong?*

But what if it *was*?

Is it enough to have good intentions if they result in something horrible? The question raised a terrible doubt in Charlie that silenced him completely.

"As you all might recall," Drake continued, "I originally ordered Mr. Benjamin Reduced, but Headmaster Brazenhope strongly disagreed. She used her position and the respect she commands as Headmaster to protect him. Why? It doesn't take a genius to figure it out. She, like him, is a Double-Threat—they protect each other. And look at the events of today. After I threatened Mr. Pinch with Reduction, who should come to his aid? Why, Mr. Benjamin, of course! Double-Threats protecting Double-Threats protecting Double-Threats. When does the madness end? When will sanity once again be restored to these proud halls? How many times must we be bitten before we put the tigers to *sleep*?"

The Director's voice was so confident and strong that even Charlie himself felt swayed by the man's impassioned argument. But, before he could speak, the massive doors of the High Council Chamber flew open, and a worker in a blue uniform rushed in.

"What is the meaning of this?" Director Drake thundered. "We are in a closed-door session!"

"I'm sorry to interrupt," the man replied, his voice trembling as all eyes turned toward him. "I wouldn't have come here if my news weren't of the utmost urgency."

"Then quit talking about how urgent it is and urgently tell us what we need to know!"

"Slagguron is on the move."

Frantic talking erupted from the assembled crowd as they debated the meaning of this unwelcome news.

"Quiet! Quiet!" Director Drake demanded, cutting through the chatter. "Where's he headed?"

The man struggled to steady his nerves. "Here. If Slagguron doesn't deviate from his present course, he'll arrive at the Nightmare Division within the hour."

· CHAPTER FIFTEEN ·
INVASION OF THE NAMED

The steel walls of the Chamber of Intelligence, nestled deep in the heart of the Nightmare Division, were covered in monitors that showed terrible images of Slagguron's destructive path as he raced through the Earth's crust, knocking down bridges and buildings in his ferocious wake. Charlie, watching from the back of the room with his friends, was amazed by the sheer volume of dirt that was being moved violently aside to allow Slagguron's passage.

"Good lord, he's fast," Rex said, eyeing the large central monitor. A white dot represented the Lord of the Nether's progress as he traveled with blistering speed across a satellite map of the United States.

"Are we certain he's headed here?" Director Drake asked, a light sheen of nervous sweat glistening on his upper lip. "His path will take him through Las Vegas—

maybe that's where he's planning to stop."

"And do what? Gamble?" Rex rolled his eyes. "No, he's coming here. The Named must've found out we were hunting them down and decided to hit us before we hit them. It's what I'd do."

Director Drake turned to William. "General Dagget, what's your recommendation?"

"We need to evacuate immediately."

"Evacuate?" Rex groaned. "Oh, come on—you can't be serious. You mean you wanna run?"

"Of course not, and I don't appreciate the implication. We will fight, but not trapped in here where Slagguron can crush us like a tin can. Our one advantage is that we know he's coming, thanks to the tracking device placed by my son."

Theodore was startled by the unexpected praise. "You hear that?" he whispered to Charlie. "He called me his son right in front of everybody."

"He sure did," Charlie replied with a smile.

"No," William continued. "We're going to clear out and when Slagguron strikes, he'll just be attacking an empty building. Then we'll portal back and hit him from aboveground, where he's not expecting it."

Rex nodded and Charlie could tell the cowboy was impressed with the plan. Director Drake turned to an aide. "Start the evacuation."

Blue lights began to flash throughout the facility, and teams of Nethermancers sprang into action, rushing to other areas of the Division to begin portaling out personnel.

"What about the civilians?" Tabitha asked Drake.

"Civilians?"

"The ones up there." She nodded to the ceiling. "If we're fighting above ground, the people in the zoo are going to get slaughtered."

The zoo! It had been so long since Charlie had entered the Nightmare Division through anything but a portal that he had completely forgotten it was actually built underneath the San Diego Zoo. He had once asked Rex why that was, but Rex had just shrugged. "Dunno. Maybe because folks are used to hearing all kinds of strange growls and noises in a zoo, so they wouldn't think twice if they get an earful of one of our critters."

Charlie wasn't sure that that was the real reason, but right now it didn't matter. If they didn't do something quickly, *feeding time at the zoo* was about to take on a whole new meaning.

"Point well taken," Director Drake said to Tabitha. "Take a squad up there and clear the area."

"Right away." She rushed out of the room.

"There he goes," William grunted, pointing to a monitor that showed an aerial view of Las Vegas.

"Just look at that destruction."

Streets buckled as something massive tunneled beneath them. The fake Statue of Liberty that adorned the front of the New York, New York, casino toppled into traffic. Cars slid into buildings; buses flipped onto their sides. Even though the video had no sound, Charlie could see pedestrians screaming as they dived to the ground to avoid the mayhem.

"Oh no," Violet moaned. "Those poor people."

They watched in horror as Slagguron passed beneath the black pyramid of the Luxor Hotel, shattering every window in the place. Glass fell to the pavement like rain. William turned to Director Drake.

"We need to alert Camp Pendleton."

The Director nodded. "Agreed."

"Wait, you're gonna call the military?" Rex shook his head in disbelief. "That's a death sentence!"

"For Slagguron?" Charlie asked.

"No, kid—for the *military*. They'll just get in our way and he'll have a field day tearing them apart."

"They're going to show up eventually," William countered. "They tend to notice little things like a giant monster running amok."

"I suppose." Rex sighed heavily. "Well, if they're coming, you better tell 'em to bring everything they've got—no sense in them being here if they're outgunned.

And you better tell 'em to hurry."

Charlie glanced back at the central monitor. Slagguron had left Las Vegas far behind and was now entering California. If he kept up that astonishing speed, he would be in San Diego within minutes. "What can we do to help?" he asked Rex.

"Help? Only way you can help is by gettin' out of here so we can do our jobs."

"No way!" Theodore shouted. "You didn't want to run and neither do we!"

"This isn't kid stuff anymore. School's out! Class dismissed! Now shoo!"

"He's right," Brooke said. "We really should go. We'll just be in the way."

Charlie knew Rex was right. They'd never been in a battle like this before and would probably just end up getting hurt or killed . . . and yet he couldn't bear the thought of missing out on the action.

"We're staying," Charlie said. "Or at least I am. I can't speak for anyone else."

Rex shook his head. "Kid, I don't have time for this. I seriously don't."

"Don't worry about us. We'll be fine."

"I thought I told you to stop saying stuff like 'we'll be fine' when you have *no idea* what you're talking about!"

And that was when they felt the vibration.

It was weak and distant at first, a faraway thrumming, like a train that was still miles down the track.

"That's him," William said. "Banisher Henderson, grab your squad and go."

"All right." Rex turned to Charlie. "You get outa here—I'm serious. Promise me, Charlie."

"I promise."

"Why don't I believe you?" With a shake of the head, Rex ran off to join the adults under his command.

The thrumming noise grew louder as the entire complex began to shake violently. Equipment fell from shelves; overhead lights sparked and then went out.

Charlie glanced at the main monitor. Slagguron was almost on top of them. "We better go," he said with a sigh.

"You sure?" Theodore asked.

Charlie nodded.

"Then hurry!" Brooke yelled. "Or it'll be too late!"

With one wave of his hand, Theodore created a portal to the 1st Ring.

That vibrating sound filled the world, and suddenly the room beneath them exploded upward with such force that it knocked them through the open gateway and into the Nether, where they landed in a pile on the hard, bluish sand.

Charlie turned back just in time to see Slagguron hurtle up from the dark, earthen depths like a gigantic great white shark. With a roar, the Named creature punched a massive hole all the way through the underground facility, his slick gray body rushing past like a freight train.

"Wow," Theodore muttered.

Then, to everyone's shock, Slagguron was quickly followed by Barakkas, Verminion, and a flying, scuttling, snapping host of deadly creatures from the Nether.

"It's all of them," Brooke gasped. "Every single Named on Earth."

"Close the portal!" Charlie shouted. "Close it now before they see us!"

With a wave of his hand, Theodore slammed the gateway shut. Instantly, the Nether went silent and still. No one moved until Brooke finally struggled to her feet, brushing off sand.

"Good job, Theo."

Theodore blushed. "Thanks. It was nothing, really. Just a quick little portal." He shrugged, obviously pleased with himself, then turned to Charlie. "So . . . when are we going back?"

"What?" Brooke shouted. "We're not going back

there, are we? We promised Rex!"

"I promised him we would leave," Charlie replied. "I never said we wouldn't go back."

"What are you, a politician? You know they don't want us there and for good reason! We could all be killed!"

"Or we could save people," Theodore countered. "You saw how many creatures were attacking. All of them! This is it, their endgame. They mean to totally wipe us out—the Nightmare Division might not even exist when they're through. We gotta do what we can, no matter what. Come on, Charlie, you agree with me, right?"

Charlie considered. It was truly a tough choice:

If they went back to fight, they could certainly be killed, no question about it. But this was an all-or-nothing attack on the Division from the army of the Nether. They had to do what they could, didn't they? They had skills—pretty good ones, actually. Why waste them? And yet . . . could he really stand to have the deaths of his friends on his head? If he chose to go back and fight, they would follow.

Was that really a choice he could make for them?

"Well?" Brooke demanded.

"We're going back," Violet said softly.

Everyone turned to her. She'd been so quiet that

Charlie had forgotten she was even there.

"You sure, Violet?" Charlie asked.

She nodded. "Tabitha was right. This isn't going to be contained in the Division. The fight's going to happen above ground, in the zoo. There will be school groups there, babies and their parents. They'll need our help."

"I don't understand you," Brooke protested. "Just a little bit ago you were telling me that you felt yourself slipping away, that the warrior part of you was taking over and you hated it. Now you want to go and fight?"

Violet looked up at the older girl with a new hardness in her eyes; Charlie was shocked by the intensity of it.

"I won't let another kid get taken from their parents . . . or another parent get taken from their kid. I won't see that happen again."

Again? Charlie wondered what Violet was talking about. Sure, his parents had been taken from him by Verminion, but she hadn't been there to witness it. He couldn't figure out what had gotten her all worked up.

Unless . . .

"Are you talking about your mother?" he asked quietly.

Violet didn't respond. Finally, she nodded almost imperceptibly.

"You said she died. How did she die?"

Violet's eyes grew watery, but she never lost her composure. "I had a nightmare."

I had a nightmare.

The weight of those four words rested heavily on Charlie's heart, and he suddenly understood so much more about his friend. Her mother hadn't just died, she had been killed. And not just killed, she had been killed by a monster from one of Violet's nightmares.

The guilt must be terrible, Charlie thought. It wasn't her fault—she'd been just a child, there was nothing she could have done to control or prevent it. And yet he knew that if it had happened to him, he wouldn't have been able to carry on.

"I'm going back to fight," Violet said. "I'm going back there to help those families. You can come with me or you can stay, but I need you to open a portal. Will you do that for me?"

"Sure," Charlie replied. "Definitely. And I'm going with you. In fact, I'd say it's time for some payback."

Theodore broke into a huge grin. "Time for some payback! Yes! That's the way I roll, baby! Yeee-hah!"

· CHAPTER SIXTEEN ·
PAYBACK

The San Diego Zoo had turned into a war zone. The first thing Charlie noticed as he stepped through the portal was the sound: a cacophony of screams and screeches and the metallic grinding of heavy machinery. The U.S. military had already begun to arrive; tanks rolled through Tiger River and Sun Bear Forest while warplanes screamed overhead.

It didn't matter.

Just as Rex had predicted, the monsters of the Nether tore through them as if they didn't even exist.

Barakkas, ten stories of thickly muscled, blue-skinned rage, pickcd up armored vehicles and threw them, as if they were as light as sandbox toys, into the approaching troops with his one good hand, knocking them down like bowling pins.

Slagguron, meanwhile, exploded from the ground in a fury of dirt and metal, exposing the ruins of the Nightmare Division directly below. Then, like a whale doing a belly flop, he slammed back into the earth, crushing everything beneath him with his astonishing bulk before disappearing into the ground once again to repeat the devastating process.

And Verminion, easily the size of a baseball diamond, scuttled forward on his crablike legs, while hundreds of rockets detonated harmlessly on the back of his thick shell. His one giant claw snapped through hastily assembled barricades like butter.

And those were just the Named monsters.

The regular Class 5s were quickly overwhelming the desperate ground troops with their sharp teeth and deadly pincers. In a surreal twist, spindly pink flamingos, long-necked giraffes, and leaping gazelles—freed from their habitats by the destruction—ran frantically through the attacking Nethercreatures. Overhead, Netherbats swooped down on jetfighters, tearing them from the sky and hurling them to the ground in massive fireballs. The big cats from the lion and tiger areas squared off against a herd of Netherstalkers and were quickly torn to pieces—there was absolutely no question who was king of the jungle here.

To Charlie, it didn't seem real.

Before today he'd only seen these vicious creatures roaming the vastness of their fiery lairs or wandering through the Rings of the Nether—but never like this; out here, in the open, in the daylight, with regular people around . . . or at least the ones the Nightmare Division had yet to evacuate.

"No!" Brooke suddenly yelled, startling Charlie out of his stupor.

He turned to see a screaming class of third graders running away as the shadow of a tank, flung by Barakkas, descended upon them. Just before it landed, a huge portal snapped open above the school group, allowing the tank to fall through and slam harmlessly into the Nether.

Charlie looked around and was surprised to discover that the portal had been opened by Tabitha. She was working so fast and so furiously that she'd already closed that portal and opened a new one to protect a zoo worker from a leaping Dangeroo.

"Duck!" Violet shouted.

Charlie ducked just as Violet threw her ax in his direction—the blade came so close to his head that it chopped off several hairs. He spun around to see the weapon now buried in the skull of a Silvertongue. The vicious beast had been a heartbeat away from using its scorpionlike stinger to spear a mother who had thrown herself in front of her little girl.

"Awesome!" Charlie shouted, but Violet rushed past without answering.

She yanked the blade from the dead Silvertongue, then waded into battle against a Hag with a calm, cool detachment that would have seemed eerie to Charlie if he hadn't recognized it in himself. It was the same distance that always came over him when his skill as a Banisher took over.

As he followed Violet into the fray, he was thrilled to see elite squads of Nethermancers and Banishers in action all around him. They swung their weapons and opened portals with such astonishing skill and grace that they made the regular soldiers appear to be moving in slow motion.

"Look out!" Charlie shouted at Theodore. The young Nethermancer—who had just opened up a portal in front of a Netherbat, forcing it to fly into the 1st Ring, where it snapped its head on a rocky outcropping—spun around to see a group of Acidspitters rushing up behind him. Theodore opened a portal beneath them, causing them to tumble into the darkness of the Nether.

"Thanks for the warning!" the tall, skinny boy shouted.

"Don't mention it!"

Charlie turned and swung his rapier at a Nether-stalker that was scuttling toward a zoo security guard. The creature fell to his blade and Charlie thought for one wonderful, shining moment, *We can do this—we can actually win this!*

And then reality set in.

Rex had told him that Banishers needed courage to do their job, which meant that the longer the odds, the stronger a Banisher could become in facing them. But didn't there come a point when the odds were just impossible? As hard and as brilliantly as everyone around him fought, Charlie knew that they were hope-lessly outnumbered by the Class-5 monsters of the Nether. When you added in the Named, it was clearly a losing battle.

People were dying: soldiers, Banishers and Nether-mancers, even some civilians who were just trying to enjoy a peaceful day at the zoo. There was nothing fun about this battle, only fear and destruction. Charlie glanced over and saw Rex and Tabitha facing off against Barakkas. Tabitha was trying to use a portal to trip the great beast, while Rex prepared to spring with his short sword—but Barakkas was too fast for them and they were quickly flung away like rag dolls, tum-bling violently through the air to land in Gorilla Tropics.

"Are you all right?" Charlie screamed.

"Yeah!" Rex called back. "We're fine, kid! Now forget about us and pay attention!"

"Will do!"

And that's when Barakkas noticed Charlie. The great beast laughed deeply.

"Well, if it isn't my old friend, Charlie Benjamin!" His swordlike talons were clenched around a tank, which he crushed effortlessly as he spoke. "So, what do you think, boy? Are you not surprised? Are you not *amazed* to see us in full, glorious action?" His massive hooves sparked fire as he strode across the stone embankment of the crocodile pen.

"It's . . . pretty amazing," Charlie said, fending off a Netherleaper. "I wasn't sure you were still alive."

Barakkas laughed again, long and loud and cheerlessly. "It was close, I'll give you that. Your trickery those many months ago very nearly cost the lives of Verminion and me, but here we are, as strong and deadly as ever, ready to put an end to your pitiful tyranny! I bet you wish now you had chosen to join us, eh, Charlie Benjamin, instead of pitting us against each other? If you had, this could be the moment of your triumph instead of the moment of your death!"

Suddenly, Barakkas roared with a sound like thunder. He scooped up a fleeing elephant with his one good hand and flung the startled beast at an attack helicopter with startling precision.

The explosion was enormous.

"Aggravating little gnat!" he roared.

What are we gonna do? Charlie thought. *How can we possibly stop them?*

And that's when he noticed Pinch.

The boy (*man*—why couldn't Charlie remember?) stood twenty yards away, staring at Verminion, who was rampaging through a platoon of soldiers. Charlie had forgotten all about him in the chaos.

"Verminion!" Pinch cried out. "Look at me, you coward!"

The great beast stopped and slowly turned to him.

"You've something to say, boy?"

"I've waited a long time for this," Pinch replied, walking steadily toward the deadly Named. "You killed my parents—now I'm going to kill you."

Oh boy, Charlie thought. What was Pinch up to? Had he let the newfound discovery of his Gift go to his head?

"Edward?" Verminion said, staring at the boy curiously. The great creature's Artifact of the Nether shined blackly around his scaly neck. "Is it really Edward *Pinch*?"

Pinch nodded. "Surprised? I'm as powerful as I used to be."

"Oh, you were quite powerful indeed." Soldiers continued their useless attack on Verminion's shell—he didn't even notice. "And yet, that didn't save your parents, or your town, or your Gift, now did it?"

Charlie had forgotten how cruel the beast could be, but Pinch didn't seem to care.

"Even though I don't look it, I'm older now," Pinch said. "Older and wiser."

"Wisdom does not always come with age, Edward. Sometimes only age comes with age."

"You should consider fortune-cookie writing. You've got quite a gift."

"So did you—until they took it away."

Pinch stared at Verminion with hatred. "I can't tell you how many times I've dreamed of killing you."

"Really? How curious. I've hardly given *you* a thought, ever since you foolishly brought me to your world."

"You're the one who's about to look foolish."

"You think so? Let's find out."

With truly shocking speed, Verminion rushed at Pinch, roaring fiercely. He was like a freight train, tearing apart everything and everyone in his path. His giant claw snapped furiously, and the great bony crest of his head was fully outstretched as he strained to get his filthy jaws that much closer to the offensive, boastful little human in front of him.

Pinch held his ground.

A split second before Verminion was in striking distance, Pinch opened a portal exactly the size of the Named beast's skull. Too late to stop, the great creature's outstretched head slipped through, and—with perfect, glorious timing—Pinch snapped it closed, decapitating him in an instant. His saucer-shaped body slammed into the ground like a downed jumbo jet, shearing up grass in great green sheets, while ichor fountained from his neck in a sticky spray.

To the complete and utter shock of everyone standing there, Verminion, one of the four Named Lords of the Nether, was dead.

· CHAPTER SEVENTEEN ·
PINCH'S PLAN

"**W**hat have you done?" Barakkas roared, staring at Verminion's headless corpse. "WHAT HAVE YOU DONE, LITTLE MAN?"

Pinch stumbled back, clearly frightened, as the Named stormed toward him, massive hooves sparking showers of flame.

Charlie was surprised by the contrast between Pinch's fearlessness toward Verminion and his terror in front of Barakkas. The big difference, he decided, was the pure, personal hatred Pinch had felt toward Verminion. After all, Verminion had killed his parents and was the direct cause of his being Reduced in the first place.

"Nothing will survive my vengeance!" Barakkas screamed, advancing.

Suddenly, Slagguron burst up out of the ground in front of him, stopping the beast with his tremendous bulk. "HOLD!"

"Stand aside, Slagguron," Barakkas thundered. "They have killed Verminion. They must pay."

"No. We must leave. We have already accomplished one of our goals."

What goal is that? Charlie wondered.

The blue-skinned monster glanced up to see news helicopters flying around him, filming the incredible display. He roared at them, red eyes blazing—it was a terrifying sight.

That's it! Charlie suddenly realized. *That's their goal—fear.* Because the Named had shown themselves like this, people all around the globe could see first-hand what terrible creatures they shared their world with. There would be many nightmares tonight.

And those nightmares would open many portals, which would bring many monsters.

"We may have done one of the things we set out to do," Barakkas said, "but at a great and terrible cost!" He glanced at the still body of Verminion. "All is now lost."

"No," Slagguron replied. "There is still hope."

Hope? Charlie wondered. *Hope for what?*

"Follow me," Slagguron said. "These miserable

humans are nothing to us. We must continue as planned."

He leaped into the air and dived headfirst into the ground, leaving behind a huge tunnel. Barakkas looked around at the assembled Nethermancers and Banishers who stood, tired and bloody, in the ruins of the zoo.

"This is not over!" he thundered. "SOON, WE WILL RETURN TO RIP YOUR WORLD APART!"

The great beast grabbed the Artifact of the Nether from around Verminion's severed neck and, with terrible speed, dived into the tunnel after Slagguron, disappearing into the darkness. The rest of the monsters followed.

Almost as quickly as it had arrived, the army of the Nether was gone.

"I don't believe it," Rex said, breaking the silence. "You did it, Pinch. You actually killed Verminion."

"I did, didn't I?" Pinch said, a smile spreading across his boyish features.

The surviving Nethermancers and Banishers—exhausted, many wounded—let out a loud cheer. *"Pinch! Pinch! Pinch!"* they chanted, and someone hoisted him up into the air. Soon, he was passed from person to person in a joyful wave of adulation.

Pinch had never looked happier, and Charlie was happy *for* him.

After a lifetime of being marginalized and despised, he was now the hero of the Nightmare Division. *What an awesome feeling it must be,* Charlie thought, *to go from such a terrible low to such an incredible high.*

Even Rex, Pinch's most vocal critic, had given the boy (*man,* Charlie thought, *man, MAN!*) his due. In the shadow of Verminion's cooling corpse, Pinch was held aloft, worshipped like a dragon slayer of old.

Good, Charlie thought. *Good for him. He deserves it.*

Charlie saw only one person who did not seem pleased at the praise being showered on Pinch. The Director of the Nightmare Division stared stonily as the new hero was passed from person to person.

"Banishers! Nethermancers!" Drake shouted, his steely voice cutting through the celebration.

One by one, the adults under his command quieted.

"While it is entirely proper to thank Mr. Edward Pinch for his service to the Division—"

Service to the Division? That's an odd way to put it, Charlie thought. Service to the Division meant service to the *Director*.

"—we must remember that this is not a time for celebration. Many of our comrades have fallen on this dark day. The world is now a different place than it was when we woke up this morning. We have not, by any means, *won*. So, please, let us keep our small triumph here in perspective."

A somberness came over them. The Nethermancer holding Pinch gently set him down.

"I could not agree more, Director," Pinch replied, straightening his clothes. It struck Charlie how odd it was to hear Pinch's adult phrasing coming from what looked like a boy his own age. "This was only a minor victory. We must not be satisfied by it. Only *total* victory should be our goal." He turned to the crowd. "And that is in reach by the end of this day!"

"What?" Director Drake said, alarmed. "How can you claim something so ridiculous?"

"I have a plan," Pinch continued, "and if we follow it, the rest of the Named, as well as all the monsters of the Nether under their command here on Earth, will be dead by sundown."

Back in the shambles that had once been the High Council Chamber of the Nightmare Division, the Banishers and Nethermancers stared in amazement as Pinch finished laying out his strategy for destroying the Named.

"With the Guardian at our side, we will portal into

their new lair in the Himalayas. The monsters of the Nether will be utterly unable to defend themselves—the Guardian's aura will cripple them—and then we can dispose of the vicious creatures with absolutely no danger to ourselves."

There was silence for a moment as everyone processed Pinch's plan. Finally, Rex let out an appreciative whistle. "I gotta tell ya, Pinch, that just may be the most audacious thing I've ever heard."

"I think it's brilliant," Tabitha said. "Bringing the Guardian to Earth, using him as a weapon—it seems so obvious that I can't believe none of us ever thought of it before."

"Well, I did," Director Drake replied from his tall chair at the front of the Chamber. "But I rejected it because of the risk it poses."

"I'm afraid I don't see the risk," Pinch countered, walking toward him. "It is a bold move at a time when boldness is required."

"What you call bold, I call foolhardy. While it's true that we now know the location of the new lair of the Named—"

"Thanks to Theodore Dagget," Pinch interrupted, shooting the boy a supportive nod. Charlie was amazed: That might have been the first time Pinch had ever given credit to someone else.

"Yes, thanks to young Mr. Dagget," the Director continued, "we now know the location of their new lair, but taking the Guardian out of the Nether and bringing it to that lair is fraught with danger."

"Yeah, for the Nethercritters," Rex said. The adults around him chortled with laughter.

The Director darkened, and Charlie wondered if it was a good idea to antagonize the man like this. He seemed on edge.

"Would the Guardian's aura cripple the Named and the other monsters in their lair, allowing us to easily destroy them?" the Director asked. "Yes, it would. However, that is *if* it survives being around so many humans, which we cannot guarantee. Also, you are forgetting that taking the Guardian away from the Anomaly would leave that giant gateway unprotected, and Tyrannus would surely take advantage to cross over to Earth."

"I didn't forget that at all," Pinch replied. "We'll simply kill him as well when he arrives at the lair. Surely anyone with half a brain could have figured that out."

"I may not have the Gift like you, Mr. Pinch, but that does not mean I have *half a brain*. You are proposing that we remove the Guardian in the hopes that we can use its powers to destroy the monsters here on

Earth, but the only thing we know for certain is that, by doing so, we will allow Tyrannus to escape from the Nether."

"Yes, and so what? Verminion is dead. It's impossible for the Named to summon the Fifth now, so we're in no danger of that. The rewards far outweigh the risks."

"Well, I stand opposed," Director Drake replied. "We would be putting the Guardian in jeopardy and releasing the last of the Named on the slim hope that we can kill everything in one fell swoop. It's foolish and it's dangerous, and I won't approve it."

"I agree with the Director," William said, stepping forward, his two-handed sword gleaming brightly even in the dim light of the ruins of the Chamber.

"Now *there's* a big shockeroo," Rex muttered.

"We can't let ourselves get carried away by this . . . man, I suppose"—William waved a hand at Pinch—"just because he's having a brief moment in the sun."

Rex stood. "Look, I never liked Pinch, that's no secret. But when a man's right, he's right, and I gotta give him his due. Slagguron and Barakkas are in chaos right now after the death of Verminion, but that won't last. Now's the time to strike. With the Guardian in front of us, knocking those bad boys down will be like shootin' fish in a barrel. We saw today what these monsters'll do if we let 'em recover, so we can't let 'em recover." He turned to the assembled crowd. "Who's with me on this?"

Tabitha stood. "I am."

"So am I," Charlie said, standing as well.

"Let's do this," Violet added, also standing.

One by one, every Nethermancer and Banisher in the Chamber stood in support of Pinch and his plan. The Director and William shared a dark, troubled glance.

Suddenly, Charlie had a flash of insight:

He doesn't want *us to kill them all,* he realized with a shock. The only thing Drake cared about was staying in power, and if all the Named and their minions were dead, the need for the Nightmare Division would be gone. Without a constant, looming threat, Drake would be powerless. And, to make matters worse, Pinch would be the conquering hero, not the Director.

"So be it," Director Drake said, staring at the room full of Nethermancers and Banishers who had turned on him. "I will approve this mission, but know this: I stand by my belief that Double-Threats are too danger-ous to remain at full power, and the very fact that you are all blindly following one of them now is further evi-dence that I am right. I believe this desperate gambit will fail, and when it does, you will see that Pinch and the other Double-Threats are to blame."

"Duly noted," Pinch replied. He turned to the crowd. "While we prepare for battle, are there any volunteers to escort the Guardian from the Nether and bring it here?"

"I will," Charlie said quietly. "I've had some experience with him."

"We *all* will," Violet added, gesturing to Brooke and Theodore beside her. They both nodded. "The four of us will go and get the Guardian."

"Excellent," Pinch replied. "Do it now."

"That's a rather remarkable plan," the Headmaster said.

The Guardian sat beside her, looking healthy and powerful. It was *so* powerful, in fact, that Charlie was shocked at how easy it had been to return to the BT Graveyard—the Guardian's aura of protection extended even farther than before. Now there was a thin area around the Graveyard where portaling was possible but no Nethercreatures could enter.

"It's so good to see you again," the Guardian murmured. Charlie was happy to hear the dying rattle gone from the creature's voice—it still spoke softly, but strongly. "I've missed you all so much. Will you hold me? I would very much like to be held."

The pull of the Guardian was even more powerful now that it had regained its strength, and Charlie had to focus strongly to avoid touching it. He glanced around to see that the others were struggling as well.

"You see how much more difficult it is to resist touching the Guardian now," the Headmaster said. "Bringing him into a crowd of humans is an enormously dangerous proposition."

"That's what the Director said," Charlie replied.

"Did he? Well, for once, he is correct." She got up and began to pace about the Guardian's warship. "Leaving here and taking him with us is quite a risk. On the other hand, just in the past few hours I returned two children back to their homes on Earth—the monstrous attack earlier today had given them the most terrible nightmares. As you might expect, they were abducted and brought here by creatures of the Nether in hopes that they would kill the Guardian." She shook her head sadly. "There is nowhere truly safe for him now."

"So you agree that we should bring him to the lair of the Named?" Violet asked.

The Headmaster sighed. "My brain says yes, but my heart says no."

Charlie felt exactly the same way, but every time he had followed his heart—rescuing the child from the

Nether who turned out to be Slagguron, for instance—it had led to disaster. He was determined to follow the logical path this time.

"The potential benefit is huge," the Headmaster continued, "but taking the Guardian to Earth and freeing Tyrannus from the Nether is a colossal risk. I just don't know . . ."

"Well, Pinch seemed very sure," Charlie said, gently prodding her.

"Did he, Mr. Benjamin?" The Headmaster smiled knowingly, and Charlie immediately felt like a clumsy fool for even trying to manipulate the wise woman. "Pinch's fortunes have changed rather dramatically in the past few hours, haven't they?"

"Definitely," Theodore said. "You wouldn't believe what's going on down there—he's like a hero to everyone. It's crazy-land, trust me."

"Oh, I do. Unfortunately, the higher you go, the farther you have to fall. That is the danger of success, and it is why most people will go to great and sometimes terrible lengths to protect it."

Like the Director, Charlie thought, but he didn't say that out loud.

"So what's it going to be, Headmaster?" Brooke asked. "Should we bring him?"

The Headmaster considered, then turned to the Guardian. "What do you think, Hank? Would you like to take a trip?"

The Guardian smiled. "I'm so lonely here. I would like to make some friends."

And so it was decided.

"TRICKERY!" Tyrannus screeched, flying high above Charlie and company as they escorted the Guardian out of reach of the Anomaly so that they could portal away. "You're up to something evil, Headmaster—old Tyrannus can smell it on you, even from this far."

"We have no more quarrel with you," the Headmaster replied. "Once we are gone, the Anomaly will be unprotected and you can escape. Isn't that what you always wanted?"

"Of course!" the golden bat shrieked. "But old Tyrannus knows what you did to Verminion. He could see it with his glittery, ghastly toy!"

The Artifact of the Nether on the Named beast's finger strobed with red light from the four images engraved on it.

"You are NASTY creatures, full of deceit and wickedness, but you will not fool old Tyrannus. He knows what you're trying to do with that poisonous little Guardian, where you want to BRING him, and now so do the others!"

They can see us, Charlie suddenly realized. He turned to the Headmaster.

"A long time ago, when I wore Barakkas's bracer, I was able to look through the eyes of the other three Named who were also wearing Artifacts. If Tyrannus can see us here with the Guardian, so can Barakkas and Slagguron."

"We must hurry then," the Headmaster said grimly, "and attack before they have a chance to respond."

They raced through the Nether as quickly as the Guardian could run on its short, stubby legs. Unfortunately, they couldn't touch it to pick it up and carry it. As soon as they were out of range of the Anomaly, the Headmaster created a portal, and they all leaped through into the heart of the remains of the Nightmare Division, where they quickly reunited with their colleagues.

The moment the portal closed behind them, the Guardian's aura in the Nether faded and, with a crazy cackle of triumph, Tyrannus the Demented sailed over the ruined ships of the BT Graveyard and shot straight up and into the churning red disc of the Anomaly.

"FREE!" he shrieked with a gale of laughter.

Seconds later, he used his great, golden wings to

propel him up through the depths of the cold Atlantic before finally exploding out of the water and into the beautiful blue skies of Earth above.

After an eternity of waiting, Tyrannus, the Fourth Named, had escaped from the Nether.

· CHAPTER EIGHTEEN ·
THE FROZEN WASTES

High in the vast, frozen wasteland of the Himalayas, hidden from the prying eyes of humans, the icy lair of the Named was alive with activity. Sleet fell through a giant hole in the ceiling of the massive cavern while a blizzard raged outside, turning the sky above into an impenetrable blanket of white.

"Hurry!" Barakkas thundered at the hundreds of Nethercreatures that swarmed at his feet as he and Slagguron raced across the slippery blue sheets of ice covering every inch of their remote base of operations. "The humans are coming. We must leave immediately!"

"Why are you so fearful of them?" Slagguron asked. "Are we not Lords of the Nether?"

"I'm not fearful of *them*—it's the Guardian I fear. I felt the touch of that horrible monster a long time ago, and I'm not eager to feel it again."

"Even with the Guardian, the humans can hurt us only if they know where we are," Slagguron reasoned. "We have no reason to think they do."

"We have no reason to think they *don't*."

Suddenly, Barakkas stopped, noticing something:

The red light that issued from the Artifact of the Nether clamped around Slagguron's middle was reflected brilliantly in the polished ice of the cavern wall, but something else pulsed in the reflection as well.

A tiny spot of blue.

"What's this?" Barakkas growled, bending down to inspect the source of the light. As soon as he saw the tracking device that Theodore had planted on Slagguron's metal belt, his orange eyes went red with rage. "They've been tracking you, you fool!" He grabbed the tiny mechanical object—in his fist, it was no larger than a grain of sand—and crushed it.

"That is unfortunate," Slagguron said with a grimace. "You are right. We must leave now, before it's too late."

But it already was.

Purple portals snapped open across the lair like fireworks, allowing elite Nethermancers and Banishers to pour through—among them, Charlie and his friends.

"Do not touch the Guardian!" the Headmaster

yelled at the other humans as she ushered the tiny, frail creature into the vast cavern.

"NO!" Slagguron shrieked as soon as he laid eyes on it.

Unimaginable pain suddenly slammed through his brain, and he collapsed on the ice next to Barakkas, who was already foaming at the mouth in agony. The hundreds of Class-5 Nethercreatures around them stumbled to the frozen ground as well, completely immobilized.

"It worked!" Charlie said, staring in awe at the creatures that lay scattered around them, writhing in pain. "The Guardian laid them out!"

"Sweet!" Theodore shouted. He extended his open palm to the Guardian. "Give me five, Hank!"

The Guardian raised its hand.

"Mr. Dagget . . . ," the Headmaster warned.

"Right. No touching. Sorry, Hank." Theodore quickly withdrew his palm.

Pinch, meanwhile, walked through the lair like a conquering general, surveying the hundreds of deadly but now powerless creatures before him with smooth satisfaction. "Excellent. All is moving according to plan, just as I said it would."

He shot a glance at Director Drake, who watched the proceedings with a scowl, arms folded. "Do not be so confident, Pinch. Even the best of plans have a weakness."

"Absolutely true, which reminds me . . ." He turned to Charlie. "Please escort the Guardian out of the way, somewhere safe, so that we can begin."

"Wouldn't he be safer here with us?" Charlie asked. "Where we can keep an eye on him?"

Pinch shook his head. "Creatures of the Nether cannot hurt him—only humans can do that. We cannot take a chance that someone might touch him, accidentally or otherwise. As you well know, the urge is nearly impossible to resist."

"Okay." Charlie kneeled down beside the delicate creature. "Will you come with me, Hank? I'll take care of you."

"Yes, Charlie." The Guardian followed him toward a winding pathway that led out of the main chamber.

"Oh, Mr. Benjamin," the Headmaster called after him. Charlie turned back. "Return quickly please—without delay." Her expression was stern and knowing.

Charlie nodded. "No problem." Even the Headmaster was afraid that he might be overcome by the desire to lay a hand on the gentle creature. They left the main chamber and walked into a small, dark vestibule at the end of an icy hallway."

"Do you think you'll be okay here?"

The Guardian nodded, its wide eyes shining brightly in the gloom. "I think so. You are kind."

"Thank you. So are you."

"Will you hold me? It would be so wonderful to be held."

"I can't. You *know* that."

The Guardian sighed in a remarkably human way. "I know. It just would be so nice for once."

Charlie smiled at him.

"Mr. Benjamin!" a voice rang out, echoing down the icy hallway. It was the Headmaster. "We are waiting!"

"Just stay here, Hank," Charlie said, "and when it's all over, I'll come back and get you."

The Guardian nodded. "Be safe, Charlie Benjamin."

"You, too."

Charlie took one last look at the gentle creature— so small against the vastness of the dark, icy walls that surrounded it—and then headed back to the main chamber to begin the process of destroying the creatures of the Nether.

"I hate this," Violet whispered as the Banishers and Nethermancers spread out across the cavern, waiting on Pinch's command to begin the assault.

Charlie knew what she meant. It was one thing to

kill a monster while it was attacking you—that was self-defense, after all—but it was another thing entirely to kill it as it lay there, defenseless.

It might not *be* wrong, but it sure *felt* wrong.

"I know exactly what you mean," Charlie whispered back. "I get that it's necessary—I mean, after what happened today at the zoo, it's hard not to—but it just doesn't seem right, somehow."

Violet nodded in agreement. "At least Theodore seems happy."

Charlie glanced over at him. Sure enough, the tall, skinny boy did seem happy. He was clearly excited to be there in the presence of his father, ready and eager to demonstrate his skill. Of course, as a Nethermancer, he wasn't the one who had to land a killing blow.

"Nethermancers, listen please," Pinch said walking among them. He wore a parka over his T-shirt to blunt the biting cold, and it dwarfed his small, boyish body. "With the exception of the two Named, you will systematically open a portal beneath all of the remaining Nethercreatures and return them to the 5th Ring."

"You don't want to kill them?" William asked, his breath coming out in great, frozen clouds.

"Of course not. You know we kill only when there is no alternative."

Charlie could easily remember the exact day in

Beginning Banishing when Rex taught them about the Rule of 3's. For every monster you killed on Earth, three of them immediately spawned in the Nether. However, if you simply returned them to the Nether without killing them, no new monsters would spawn. That was the whole reason for taking the trouble to Banish the Nethercreatures back through portals to begin with, even though it would have been much easier just to destroy them outright.

"I know the rule," William replied, annoyed. "This isn't my first day at the dance. But this isn't the time for delicacy. Now that you got us all here, we need to move fast and hard and get this thing done for good."

"We will," Pinch said. "But we must also be smart. Don't worry, William, you'll get to quench your thirst for blood today. We may be returning the regular monsters to the Nether, but the Named must still be destroyed."

The Named.

Charlie glanced over at Barakkas and Slagguron, curled up in pain, unable to move. He knew that they were vicious and deadly and would kill every human in the place if they had half a chance . . . but there was still something so pathetic about the way they were just lying there, spread out across the ice, defenseless. It was clear what had to be done, and yet—Charlie didn't want to do it. He just wished he could shut his eyes tightly and disappear.

Everything was moving way too fast. He was still just a student, for crying out loud! All his friends were. The good times he'd had with them—exploring the nooks and crannies of the Nightmare Academy; swimming in the warm, clear ocean beyond; and having playful swordfights on the beach—now seemed like a distant, hazy memory.

This was serious business, time to *grow up*, as Mama Rose said—and he didn't like it.

Not one bit.

"All right, Nethermancers," Pinch yelled, his voice echoing across the massive cavern. "Let's begin!"

With grim determination, they began opening fiery purple portals beneath the crippled Class-4 and -5 monsters lying on the icy floor of the lair, allowing them to fall harmlessly into the Nether. Theodore easily kept up with the adult Nethermancers. Charlie noticed him glance over at his father for some sign of acknowledgment or approval. After a couple of tries, he finally caught his dad's eye.

William shot him a wink.

Good, Charlie thought. *Finally.*

As the Nethermancers went about their business, Violet turned to Brooke. "Why don't you get on out there?"

"Me? What are you talking about?"

"To help them."

Brooke seemed confused. "How? You know I can't portal anymore."

"You can, Brooke. I know you can, and so do you. You've done it before. Now go on."

"Well . . . okay. I'll try."

Unsure, Brooke walked out and struggled to open a portal. It didn't come quickly or easily, but to her astonishment she finally managed to open a small one beneath a Class-4 Acidspitter.

It fell soundlessly into the Nether.

With a grin, Brooke glanced back at Violet, who gave her a supportive smile. Newly confident, Brooke went back to work opening another portal while Charlie and the Headmaster joined Tabitha and the rest of the Nethermancers as they solemnly continued to return the remaining monsters to the Nether. There seemed to be a million of them. Everyone was so focused on the task at hand that no one even noticed someone was missing from the main cavern:

The Director of the Nightmare Division was gone.

The Guardian saw the long shadow approach from the hallway, creeping along the icy walls like an oil slick.

"Hello," the gentle creature said. "Have you come to see me?"

"Yes," Director Drake whispered, his eyes pools of black in the dim light.

"Are you a nice man?"

"I am."

"Good," the Guardian said. "It's so lonely here. And so cold. Will you hold me?"

"I will."

The Director enfolded the small creature in his long arms, pressing his bare cheek against the top of its fragile head.

"Oh, thank you," the Guardian said, smiling, as color began to leach out of its thin skin. "It's so nice to be held after so long—living in the cold and the dark of the Nether. Are you a kind man, like Charlie Benjamin?"

The Director didn't answer.

The Guardian's wide, white eyes began to grow yellow as sharp ribs revealed themselves at odd angles in its sinking chest. Its breathing became shallow and ragged.

"Are you my friend?" the Guardian asked, a little tentatively now.

A cold wind blew down the frigid hallway as the blizzard raged high overhead. The Director, silent as a tomb, squeezed the tiny creature more tightly, pressing the poison of his skin against it and holding it there, even as it started to struggle.

A terrible awareness began to dawn in the dying creature's eyes.

"Oh my," it croaked softly. "You're *not* my friend, are you?"

"No," the Director whispered. "I'm afraid I'm not."

The Guardian sighed then and whispered only three more words:

"Alone . . . always alone."

It gasped once, then once more . . . and then finally was still.

· CHAPTER NINETEEN ·
THE WORM TURNS

While the Nethermancers continued their work, the Banishers grouped around the massive, immobilized bodies of the Named. Charlie stood next to Violet—mere feet from Barakkas's tough, blue hide—while Rex and William took a position by Slagguron.

"We will do this as quickly and painlessly as possible," Pinch said, drawing his sickle. It gleamed a startling blue. "I know many of you find this distasteful. We are not assassins, certainly, but sometimes dark deeds must be performed so that the light of peace can shine."

The light of peace? Charlie thought. *What kind of crazy talk is that?* It was almost as if he were already campaigning for the job of Director of the Nightmare Division.

"After we complete our duty," Pinch continued, "we will arise tomorrow in a safer world than the one we awoke in today." Pinch raised his sickle in his small hand.

Following his lead, the other Banishers, including Rex and William, raised their weapons.

"Banishers," Pinch said, "on my command—"

Charlie glanced at Violet, sick to his stomach. "I know," she whispered, obviously just as upset as he was. "Let's just get it over with."

Charlie nodded. "Yeah. Okay."

He raised his rapier, she raised her ax.

Pinch began to count down to the attack. *"One . . . two—"*

Suddenly, Barakkas twitched.

The Banishers glanced at each other, nervous.

"Am I seeing things?" Violet asked, "or did he just—"

Another spasm ran through the body of the mighty Named, causing a talonlike finger to curl up under his one good claw, ripping a giant trough in the ice beneath.

"He . . . he moved," Charlie said.

"Uh-oh," Rex muttered. "This is definitely not good."

Barakkas opened his eyes and looked over at the

humans. "Apparently, no one has checked on the Guardian," he said with a grin. Then he leaped to his hooves with such thunderous force that ice fell from the cavern ceiling, raining down like broken glass on the monsters and humans far below.

Slagguron—also recovered—quickly raised up to his full height. He towered high above everyone, body curled into an *S* shape, dark eyes blinking, as the other creatures of the Nether regained consciousness around him.

Just like that, the humans were surrounded by fully awake, fully furious monsters ready to seek their revenge.

"This can't be happening," Tabitha said.

William turned to Pinch with fury in his eyes. "You've killed us all."

"No," Pinch protested. "This . . . this isn't part of the plan . . ."

And that was when the monsters attacked.

Slagguron threw himself down onto the ice with stunning force, crushing humans and creatures alike under his awesome weight. Barakkas stomped the ground with his mighty hooves, fangs bared, eyes wild with rage.

"Now we get our REVENGE!" the massive beast thundered, hot spittle flying from his mouth. "Now you will all PAY!"

"Retreat!" the Headmaster screamed. "Portal away! We cannot win this!"

As hundreds of newly risen monsters descended upon them, the Banishers swung into action, trying to protect the Nethermancers, who frantically struggled to open portals so that they could all escape.

"You just do your best, sweetheart," Rex said calmly to Tabitha, his lasso lashing and short sword flashing at the incoming creatures. "I'll keep 'em off ya long as I can."

While she worked at creating a portal in the midst of the chaos, Pinch stumbled through the vast cavern in something like shock.

"This is impossible," he wailed. "My plan was fool-proof!" Pinch grasped at the Banishers and Nethermancers, desperate for their forgiveness and acceptance, as they fought valiantly to save themselves and their comrades. "I couldn't have known it would end like this," he pleaded. "Remember, I killed Verminion. I'm a hero . . ."

But there was neither forgiveness nor acceptance in anyone's eyes as they pushed him away and continued to fight their doomed battle.

Amid the screams and shrieks, Theodore's father, William, ran from the main lair to see what had become of the Guardian. He found the gentle creature in the small, icy chamber where Charlie had hidden it.

The Director was lowering its still body to the ground.

"No," William said. "What have you done?"

"Only what *had* to be done," Director Drake replied. "But surely you can see that."

William rushed up to the Guardian and pulled it from the Director's hands, hoping for signs of life—but there weren't any.

"Can you imagine if this little operation had been successful?" Drake said, as if the very possibility were incomprehensible to him. "The Double-Threats would have taken over the Division, William. They would have ruined us." He shook his head sadly. "Clearly, something had to be done."

"People are *dying* out there!"

"I know," the Director replied. "And it's terrible, it really is—but hard men must make hard choices, and sometimes sacrifices are necessary to protect the greater good."

"The greater good? My *son* is out there!"

Suddenly, Theodore ran into the chamber. "Dad!" he yelled, "I'll portal us out!"

With a wave of his hand, Theodore created a portal . . . and that was when he noticed the lifeless

Guardian in his father's arms.

"What are you doing?" Theodore asked softly, backing away, horrified.

"No," William replied. "It's not what you think . . ."

"You *touched* him? He can't be touched—you know that. We all know that! Everyone knows that!"

William shook his head. "You don't understand—"

"How could you?" Theodore screamed. "My best friends are in this fight! Because of you, I don't even know if Charlie and Violet are still alive! I don't know if *anyone's* alive!"

Just then, a new sound echoed down the hallway and throughout the cavern. It was the bright and lunatic laugh of something monstrous.

"GREETINGS!" a booming voice cried out, "and many great hellos!"

Tyrannus flapped down on his great, golden wings, his wild eyes rolling crazily in their sockets. "Yum, yum, yum! I thought I missed all the fun!"

Oh no, Charlie thought as he fought off a Dangeroo. *It just doesn't end, does it?*

Now there were three Named in the giant lair.

Rapier flashing, Charlie began to race around, desperate to find his friends before Tyrannus joined in the frenzy, but the air was thick with swirling snow and the ground was slick with monster blood. Through the freezing haze, he could see some portals winking into existence as others disappeared, taking with them desperate Banishers and Nethermancers. People were either escaping from this death trap or falling prey to the monsters of the Nether.

As Charlie fought, he ran down a mental checklist, trying to figure out where he'd last seen his friends. He knew Rex and Tabitha were working as a team near Slagguron, but that had been a while ago. He had no idea if they were still in the lair or if they'd been able to make their escape.

Please let them have gotten away, he wished desperately.

As for the Headmaster, Charlie had glimpsed her brilliant blue staff light up the far reaches of the frozen cavern while she cut down vast armies of attacking Nethercreatures. The last he'd seen of her, she was so swarmed by monsters that only her staff was visible. Whether she had survived or not, whether it was even *possible* to survive the terrible odds she faced, was anyone's guess.

He was little more certain about Violet and Brooke. While he was fighting off a Hag, he thought he saw Brooke create a portal that both girls had escaped through—but he wasn't a hundred percent sure. They were far away and his eyes played tricks on him in the crazy reflections of this icy maze.

And Theodore—Charlie had seen him run off a while ago, chasing after his father. But where were they now?

Be safe, Theodore, he thought fiercely, willing it to be true. *Be alive.*

From somewhere behind him, he could hear Pinch wandering through the madness, yelling about how sorry he was, about how none of this was really his fault. Charlie didn't know whether or not that was true, and frankly he didn't really care—not now, anyway.

Now was the time for survival.

"Pinch!" Charlie cried out. "Where are you? If you're hurt, say so and I'll come get you and portal us out!"

"They all hate me now," Pinch wailed pitifully in the distance. "Just like before."

"Hang on, I'm coming to find you!"

Charlie fought his way past a Class-5 Netherstalker as he headed in the direction where he thought he'd heard Pinch. In his frenzy he slipped on a frozen patch of blood and hit his head—hard—on an icy ledge. It didn't seem too bad, at first—nothing he couldn't shake off after a minute or two—but then his body began to feel distant, as if he were looking at it in a faraway mirror.

He tried to stand but his legs felt like rubber, and he slid back down to the ice.

Oh no, he thought, *I'm fainting. I can't believe it!*

And soon blackness washed over him in a warm, wet wave.

When Charlie awoke, he was all alone in the lair of the Named.

As far as he knew, the other humans were gone— those who were still alive, anyway. His head throbbed and he was fighting the urge to vomit, but he stood on shaky legs and prepared to open a portal to escape, when he heard a familiar throaty voice:

"Charlie Benjamin," Barakkas said.

Charlie turned.

Barakkas, Slagguron, and Tyrannus stood behind him like giant trolls from some ancient, evil fairy tale. Their Artifacts of the Nether gleamed brilliantly, reflected a hundred times over in the walls of ice that surrounded them.

"Yes?" Charlie replied. He was exhausted.

"It doesn't have to end like this, boy," Barakkas said pleasantly, stepping toward him. "Just because the rest of humanity will die at our hands doesn't mean you have to."

"Of course not!" Tyrannus chirped happily, flapping into the air with enthusiasm. The force of his wings sent the smaller Nethercreatures around him tumbling away. "There are no hard feelings! We are your friends, Charlie Benjamin—and friends always eat friends, don't they!"

"Friends always eat friends?" Charlie repeated. He wasn't sure he'd heard correctly. "What does that mean?"

"It means," Slagguron said, his voice a low rumble, "that Tyrannus has lost his mind."

"I have NOT!" Tyrannus shrieked. "After all, how could someone crazy clean his own ears with his tongue?"

Shockingly, he proceeded to do just that.

"Fine," Slagguron said, "but you still cannot eat the boy."

Tyrannus pouted. "Why not?"

"Because he is going to help us."

"How?" Charlie asked. "How can I possibly help you?"

Barakkas tossed something down in front of him. As big around as a water tower, it hit the ground with a tremendous *clang*, and Charlie recognized it almost immediately.

"Verminion's choker? What's that for?"

"You wore my bracer once," Barakkas said. "Which means you're the only human who has ever been able to wield an Artifact of the Nether without being destroyed."

"So?"

"So, Verminion may be dead—but you, Charlie Benjamin, can use the Artifact in his place to join us in summoning the Fifth."

Charlie's blood froze. "No . . . I thought you had to have all four Named to do that."

"We needed all four Named," Barakkas said, "because we needed all four *artifacts*. It is the artifact that is important, not the one who wields it." He nodded to the choker on the ground with his great horns.

"YOU can be the fourth Named, Charlie Benjamin."

Suddenly, Charlie understood what Slagguron had meant during the attack on the Nightmare Division when he had told Barakkas "there is still hope." Verminion's death wasn't fatal to their plans as long as they still had Charlie.

He shook his head. "I won't do it."

"Oh, you will," Barakkas replied, "or you will die."

Charlie shrugged. "Maybe. Or maybe I'll be able to portal out before that happens. Wanna see who's quicker?"

"Stop being so DIFFICULT!" Tyrannus shrieked, flapping forward. "You have to use it—you must! You're the only human who can!"

"That's not entirely true," a voice behind Charlie said.

He spun to see Pinch standing there, bloodied and bruised. Pinch smiled grimly, and the combination of world-weary eyes on such a young-looking face was, at best, disturbing. "Charlie was able to put on the Bracer because he's a Double-Threat . . . but so am I."

"No, Edward," Charlie said. "Don't do this."

"There's nothing for me here anymore," Pinch said softly. "They all hate me now—everyone at the Nightmare Division. They blame me for this." He gestured to the massacre that surrounded him. "I can't fault them, I suppose. I would hate me, too, if our positions were reversed."

"They'll forgive you, Edward," Charlie said. "I'm sure they will. It just might take some time."

Edward shook his head. "I may look like a child, but you *are* one, Charlie Benjamin. You have a lot to learn about people. They do not forgive and they do not forget." He craned his head up to look at Barakkas. "If I do this for you, what will you give me in return?"

"Your life," Barakkas replied with a smile. Charlie could see bits of meat hanging from his teeth. "And a place at our side. The Fifth will want you to remain here, of course, to open more portals to the Nether, to bring monsters to aid us in our fight."

"They're lying to you," Charlie said. "You know they are. After you do what they want, they'll kill you."

"So what? I have nothing to live for anyway."

The higher you go, the Headmaster had said, *the farther you have to fall.*

Pinch, who had started out as one of the most powerful Double-Threats ever born, had spent most of his life as a miserable, broken man after being Reduced. Then, through nothing short of a miracle, he had quickly risen to dizzying heights, regaining his Gift and slaying Verminion.

To lose all that now, *again*, was simply too much for him to bear.

He reached out his hand—smooth and small—and touched Verminion's choker. It shrank down to a size that would fit him perfectly.

"Please don't," Charlie said. "It's not too late, Edward. You can still make things right."

"Grow up, Charlie," Pinch said, unhinging the Artifact of the Nether and fastening it around his own neck.

All four Artifacts suddenly glowed with a brightness that rivaled even the sun's.

Tyrannus cackled with glee. "Yum, yum, yum—time for the FUN!"

"Good!" Slagguron shouted, rising to his full, astonishing height. "That feels very good!"

"It does!" Pinch yelled, his face a mask of ecstasy. "I never thought something could feel so wonderful!"

"Yes, indeed!" Barakkas shouted, orange eyes now purple with unquenchable lust. "It is time!"

Charlie backed away from them, utterly heartbroken, feeling that he had failed himself, his friends, and maybe even the entire human race.

"Let us begin, my friends," Barakkas thundered, "and use all our strength to summon the Fifth!"

The ritual of summoning began.

PART
· IV ·
THE FIFTH

CHAPTER TWENTY

PEARL

The Artifacts of the Nether shined so brightly that Charlie had to close his eyes to avoid being blinded. He knew he should use this opportunity to portal away, to escape, but how could he leave before seeing what was to come?

"Let it flow!" he heard Barakkas roar. "Does it not feel wonderful? Is this not what we have been missing all our lives?"

"Yes!" Pinch shouted deliriously. "Wait—I see a doorway in front of me—a bright and shining light!"

"Open it!" Slagguron commanded. "That is the doorway to the Fifth. We must all open it so the Fifth can come through!"

"The Fifth is KIND," Tyrannus screeched. "The Fifth is MERCIFUL!"

A loud vibration rumbled through the cavern, and

Charlie could feel its steady pulse throbbing all the way into his soul. Heat baked him from all sides, melting the ice, turning it into steam that blasted his face. The light was now so intense that, even with his eyes closed, it penetrated, driving itself into his brain like a red-hot spike.

"The door is open!" Pinch shrieked.

"Come through!" Slagguron shouted.

"The Fifth is coming!" Tyrannus cackled, then: "THE FIFTH IS HERE!"

The brilliant light began to dim. That intense thrumming noise receded into the distance, and the heat that enveloped Charlie started cooling. Soon, everything was quiet in the lair of the Named, except for the sound of running water and the patter of many feet as the creatures of the Nether scuttled fearfully away.

Full of dread, Charlie opened his eyes.

The Fifth stood in the center of the lair, flanked on all sides by the three remaining Named and Pinch. Like the Guardian, it wasn't what Charlie expected at all.

The Fifth was a woman, roughly eight feet tall— much larger than a human but dwarfed by the towering Named that surrounded her. She was incredibly striking, with an alien beauty that Charlie found uncomfortably appealing. Her skin was a deep, flawless scarlet—the color of blood—and her wide catlike eyes glowed like brilliant purple jewels. She had four arms with fingers that ended in sharp, precisely manicured nails the exact color of her eyes. Her legs were long and her body was full of alluring, womanly curves. The hair on top of her head was silver and wild and seemed to move on its own, against the wind, as if it were a separate living thing.

"Hello, children," she said in a voice as sweet as honey and as smooth as rich cream. "I've waited so long to see my babies."

The Named bowed. Charlie noticed that Pinch followed their lead and bowed as well.

The Fifth studied them with exquisite slowness, as elegant and regal as a goddess. Finally, she asked: "Where is Water?"

"Water, my lady?" Barakkas replied, head still bowed.

"Call me 'Pearl.'" Charlie thought he detected a hint of amusement in her voice. "I'm looking for the Crab—the Lord of Water. I do not see him."

"Ah, you mean Verminion," Barakkas said, raising his eyes to her.

She nodded. "Yes, Verminion—is that what you call him?"

"We do."

"Interesting." She glanced toward Slagguron. "I see here the Worm, the Lord of Earth—"

"Welcome," Slagguron replied, his voice a throaty rumble.

She turned toward Tyrannus. "And here is the Bat—the Lord of Air."

Tyrannus flapped his giant wings. "I fly high and make humans DIE!"

"And then there is *you*," she continued, nodding to Barakkas. "My sweet Lord of Fire."

As if to show off, Barakkas stomped a giant hoof on the bare rock of the cave, creating a shower of flame. "Fire, indeed!" he said gleefully.

"So, before me stand the Lords of Earth, Air, and Fire, but not Water. Why is this?"

"The Lord of Water is dead," Barakkas replied. "Killed by this human." He pointed toward Pinch, spitting out the word *human* as if it tasted terrible in his mouth.

The Fifth slowly swiveled her head to look at him.

Charlie, watching from his hiding spot behind the rock, knew that Pinch must have been desperate to run—he certainly was—but Pinch held his ground.

"Edward Pinch," she said.

"You know my name?"

"Oh, yes. I know all my babies . . . and you are now

one of my babies. I hope you like that."

Edward smiled. "I do. Thank you."

"You can kill him, if you like," Barakkas said dismissively. "Now that you are summoned, we have no more use for him."

She turned slowly to Barakkas. "I can kill him? How very kind of you to give me permission, Fire. How very *generous* of you."

Barakkas seemed to grow distinctly uncomfortable. "I didn't mean it that way. You, of course, rule us all, and I would never think to suggest that—"

With the slightest, most subtle flick of her top right hand, Barakkas was consumed in an inferno of flame. It burned so brightly and so hotly that the rock beneath him melted. Moments later, the fire disappeared, leaving behind what looked like a statue of Barakkas made entirely of ash.

The Fifth pursed her lips and blew on it.

The ashen statue collapsed, blooming outward, filling the lair with a thick, choking cloud of smoke. And, just like that, Barakkas, the First Named Lord of the Nether, born of Fire, was gone.

Slagguron and Tyrannus stepped back, shocked.

"Pearl loves all her children," the Fifth said with a hint of a smile. "But sometimes children need to be punished."

Charlie couldn't believe his eyes. Even Pinch seemed stunned by the casual suddenness of Barakkas's fiery death.

"We would never oppose you," Slagguron said gravely, head bowed. "Not now—not until the end of time."

"Oh, I know you wouldn't," the Fifth replied with exaggerated earnestness, as if nothing in the world were more important to her than soothing Slagguron's concerns. "At least not intentionally. The problem, of course, is that you simply cannot help yourselves. It is—how should I say?—in your natures to seek dominance and control. It's what you were born to do. That's why you naughty boys haven't always played nicely with one another."

"Please," Slagguron said. "You must believe me. You have my word that we would never—"

But, before he could finish, she flicked a finger at him from her lower left hand. His gray skin instantly turned to stone, and he froze where he stood. Then, with another flick of her finger, he shattered as if struck by an earthquake and tumbled to the ground in a great tidal wave of sand.

It took less than three seconds for Slagguron, the Third Named Lord of the Nether, born of Earth, to lie dead.

The Fifth turned to Tyrannus.

"Hello," Tyrannus said, a nervous smile creeping across his face. "Tyrannus is so glad you—removed—those naughty Named. Like you say, they were bad boys, both of them, and they deserved their icky end!"

"Did they?" she asked mildly.

"Of course!" Tyrannus roared. "In fact, you were too kind to them! They were liars and thieves! They wanted to plunder your power!"

"But you don't?"

"Tyrannus? No! Old Tyrannus has no desire for power! He lives to serve. He wants only to be of use! Tyrannus loves his master!" The great beast grinned hopefully—it was a terrifying sight. "Does master love her Tyrannus?"

"Of course she does," the Fifth replied sweetly. "She loves all her boys equally."

"Equally?" Tyrannus repeated.

"Yes. Equal treatment for all of them."

In a frenzy of flapping wings, Tyrannus suddenly rose into the air and tried to escape through the hole in the cavern ceiling.

He didn't make it.

With a twitch of the Fifth's bottom right hand, a tornado appeared around Tyrannus, engulfing him. He struggled against the ferocious winds, but there was simply no fighting the fury of her creation. The unnatural funnel grew in intensity until Charlie could no longer see Tyrannus inside it—he had been completely consumed. Then, with the slightest of nods from the Fifth, the tornado disappeared, taking Tyrannus with it to a place from which he could not return.

Just like that, Tyrannus, the Fourth Named Lord of the Nether, born of Air, was no more.

Charlie was stunned.

It had taken all the resources of the Nightmare Division over twenty years, plus an enormous amount of luck, as well as the work of three Double-Threats, to take down just one of the Named. But now, in the space of what seemed like no more than a few heartbeats, the Fifth had utterly destroyed the remaining three.

And it didn't even seem like it required any effort.

She turned to Pinch.

"My boy. Do you love your sweet Pearl?"

"I do."

"Are you afraid of me?"

"Yes."

She nodded. "Good. I treasure honesty above all things—it is all that Pearl demands of her babies. That, and total obedience."

"I understand."

She walked to him then on her long, scarlet legs. Nearly twice Pinch's height, she towered over him, holding his gaze steadily. "You have a choice now. You can join me and seek revenge on a world that has shunned you, or you can return to that world."

"You would let me leave?" Pinch asked.

She nodded. "Of course. Pearl doesn't want any children here against their will. Their unhappiness would make her unhappy. However"—she smiled gently—"Pearl has glorious things in store for little babies who want to stay and demonstrate their love and devotion. To those that join her, Earth is a treasure chest, overflowing with meaty treats—and Pearl's little helpers can take as much as they want."

"Yes," Pinch said, staring into her jewel-like eyes. "That's what I want. I want it all."

"I know you do." She stroked his head with her four, long-fingered hands. It made Charlie shudder with revulsion. "Now, will you help Pearl by opening a portal to the Inner Circle? She has many children there that she has not seen in a long time."

"Yes."

Pinch closed his eyes and opened a giant portal to the Inner Circle of the Nether.

Charlie had seen it before. In fact, he'd opened portals to it himself in the past—much to everyone's dismay—but this was a different view entirely. He was looking into a vast courtyard, filled with Class-5 monsters busily weaving their way around twisted statuary that celebrated each of the Lords of the Nether. In all four corners stood a palace, one for every Named. The sky above was a churning cauldron of red.

The monsters in the courtyard slowly stopped what they were doing as they noticed the immense purple portal.

"Come, my babies," the Fifth said soothingly, beckoning the creatures of the Nether forward. "Come to Earth. Come to Pearl."

They raced toward her, rushing through the portal and leaving the Nether behind. Soon, she was surrounded by them, as playful as puppies, and she stroked their monstrous faces gently, with affection.

"Pearl loves her children. Pearl wants to give her babies the *world*."

As she cooed to them, hundreds more poured out of the palaces of the Named and rushed through the portal, flooding the lair. There were Netherstalkers and Ectobogs, Darklings and Hags, Dangeroos and Acidspitters, as well as many creatures that Charlie had not yet seen or even heard of.

"Come!" the Fifth said happily. "Earth is ours for the taking, babies! All are welcome!" She turned to where Charlie was hidden. "Even *you* are welcome, Charlie Benjamin."

Charlie froze.

"Come out, child. You won't be harmed."

Charlie stepped out from the rock he hid behind and entered the massive cavern. Within seconds, he found himself surrounded by monsters. They turned to him like rockets homing in on a target.

"Don't crowd him, children," the Fifth said pleasantly. Instantly, the Nethercreatures backed away, giving him plenty of room. Charlie was astonished at how quickly and completely they followed her every word. "Edward, I think you know our guest."

"Indeed," Pinch said, and Charlie knew that he was not wanted here—not by Pinch, at least.

"Would you like to join Edward and me?" she asked sweetly. "The world has enough tasty riches for us all."

"I don't think so," Charlie said.

"No?" She seemed only mildly upset, as if Charlie had simply passed on second helpings of a meal she had prepared. "No matter. You may leave, then, and let everyone know—let the *world* know—that what they have seen so far is just a tiny taste, just the slightest little bite of the doom that is about to descend upon them from Pearl and her sweet babies."

Is she messing with me, Charlie wondered, *or does she really plan to let me go?*

"With all humility," Pinch said, "Benjamin is quite powerful. He'll be the strongest foe we ever face."

We. Charlie was darkly amused by the man's choice of words—apparently, Pinch had decided that he was now an official creature of the Nether.

The Fifth seemed surprised. "Really? He's that strong, is he?" She turned to Charlie. "Are you sure you won't join us, child? Pearl's heart is large—it can contain multitudes."

"I won't join you," Charlie replied. "Never."

"Too bad." She turned to the creatures of the Nether then, many of whom were still pouring through Pinch's portal:

"Children—*destroy him.*"

It happened so fast that it was over before Charlie even realized it had started.

A wave of monsters rushed toward him, jaws snapping, pincers raised. At exactly the same moment, he opened a portal and leaped toward it. The deadly creatures washed over him in a deadly flood—

But, by then, it was too late—he was already gone.

He had escaped to the Nether.

· CHAPTER TWENTY-ONE ·
THERE'S NO PLACE LIKE HOME

In the ruins of the High Council Chamber of the Nightmare Division, Director Reginald Drake addressed the surviving Nethermancers and Banishers. The Headmaster was not present—neither were Rex, Tabitha, Charlie, Violet, or Theodore—but William, his General, stood silently by his side.

"I wish, with all my heart, that I had been wrong," Director Drake said solemnly. "I wish I could stand in front of you today, with the evil of the Named and their terrible minions a distant memory, and say to you all that I had misjudged the Double-Threats—that Edward Pinch, Headmaster Brazenhope, and Charlie Benjamin had nothing but our best interests at heart.

"Sadly, I cannot.

"We have been betrayed, ladies and gentlemen—heinously, maliciously betrayed. Why did Charlie

Benjamin poison the Guardian? Was it out of ego? Greed? We may never know. We do know, however, that he was the only one alone with that gentle creature, and that it died soon after it came into contact with him. How much did it suffer after being exposed to his poisonous human touch? Did it cry out in pain? Did it scream?

"Again, we may never know.

"And Edward Pinch? Did he intentionally lead us all to slaughter? It appears that he did. We now know that he has sided with the monsters of the Nether, and we must assume that he was in league with them all along. Why? Because he, like the other Double-Threats, seeks power above all else—and he must have felt that joining the Named was the best way to achieve it.

"Which brings us to the Headmaster.

"Who trained the Double-Threats? Who fought for them when all the voices of reason rose up in opposition to their evil ways? Who assigned them their missions and then protected them even in grave failure? Do I even need to say her name? Headmaster Brazenhope, of course—the architect of their infamy.

"These three—Edward Pinch, Headmaster Brazenhope, and Charlie Benjamin—have led us down a dark and desperate path.

"The Fifth has been summoned, and the Army of

the Nether mobilizes even as we speak here today. It is too late for regrets, and the time has passed for second chances. We can now only look to the future with clear heads and stout hearts. We must face down the terrible monsters that used to be contained—safely, if not soundly—in our nightmares.

"With thoughts of our fallen brothers and sisters forever burned into my soul and with firm resolve and strong determination, I offer myself—and General Dagget—to lead the way to a brighter future."

The Director turned to William then, who stared silently at the crowd as if lost in thought.

"General Dagget?" the Director gently prodded. "Is there anything you would like to add?"

William didn't move.

"William?"

"No," he said finally, his voice hoarse and cracking. "I think you've said it all."

The Director turned back to the crowded room.

"The age of the Double-Threat has passed, and we welcome the dawning of a bright and shining era of logic and reason. As we rebuild this great facility, I ask you to follow me, Banishers and Nethermancers— follow *us*"—he nodded to William—"as we face off against the army of the Nether and turn our backs on those who have sought to destroy us, those whom we now send into exile, those we call . . . the 'Double-Threats.'"

There was silence, followed by the sound of applause. Starting small, it soon became a thunderous roar, echoing across the great chamber. Within moments, all the surviving Banishers and Nethermancers stood, clapping furiously, showing their support for the Director—whom they had clearly so terribly misjudged—and their defiance of Charlie Benjamin and his friends.

"What does *exile* mean?" Theodore asked as he, Charlie, and Violet pitched shells off the top of the Nightmare Academy. The day was clear and the sky was a brilliant, cloudless blue, although there was a hint of chill in the air. Charlie knew it was just winter coming, but his mind crazily tried to make a connection between the loss of warmth and the death of the Guardian, which now left the Academy unprotected against the monsters of the Nether.

"I don't know what they mean by *exile*," Charlie answered. "That we're not wanted at the Division, for sure. Whether it means something more serious, like they want to arrest us or Reduce us or something . . . I have no idea. The Headmaster could probably tell us, but she's . . ." He shrugged and sighed heavily. "You know."

"She still hasn't woken up?" Violet asked.

Charlie shook his head. "Mama Rose is taking care of her in the infirmary, but her wounds were pretty serious. No one will tell me how serious."

"I never saw anyone fight so many monsters at once," Theodore said. "She's totally unbelievable."

"She really is," Violet added. "I mean, how could anyone think that she, or you"—she nodded to Charlie—"would ever want to kill the Guardian?"

Charlie shrugged. "I don't know, but they definitely blame me. I never touched him, though."

"I believe you."

"So do I," Theodore added, staring off into the jungle. A bird screeched from somewhere far below. "Because I know who the real murderer is."

Charlie and Violet turned to him, shocked.

"You do?" Charlie asked.

Theodore nodded. Charlie desperately wanted to ask who, but he waited so that Theodore could tell them when he was ready. Finally, Theodore looked at them:

"My father."

"No," Charlie said. "That can't be. He's the General—he's trying to protect the Division, not destroy it!"

"It's true," Theodore said quietly. "I caught him

red-handed. He was holding the Guardian, laying it on the ice, dead."

"Maybe you didn't see what you think you saw," Violet suggested. "I mean, everyone thinks Charlie did it and they're wrong about that."

Theodore shook his head. "I know what I saw, and what I saw is that my father is a monster."

Monster. The word hung there in the air.

"How did you escape?" Charlie asked after a moment.

"I portaled us out—me, my father, and the Director."

"And did you talk to him afterward?" Violet asked. "Your father, I mean. Maybe he has some other explanation for—"

Theodore cut her off. "I'm never talking to him again. Far as I'm concerned, I don't have a father."

Charlie wasn't sure what to say, but Violet spoke eloquently just by laying her head on Theodore's shoulder.

"Hi, guys."

Charlie glanced down to see Brooke on a platform below them, walking with her boyfriend, Geoff.

"Hey, Brooke," Charlie called back. "You guys doing all right?"

"Yeah. We're off to hang out with some friends."

"Oh. Well, have fun."

"Bye, Brooke," Violet said. "And thanks again for that portal back in the lair—you saved my life."

"Well, I wouldn't have been able to make it to begin with if you hadn't kept those monsters off me, so you saved mine, too." She smiled warmly, then she and Geoff walked off.

"What does she see in that guy?" Theodore moaned.

"I don't know," Violet replied. "He's kind of good-looking, I guess."

"Him? Are you serious? Yeah, I guess he's good-looking if you like them big and muscle-y and blond!" He snorted with laughter as if the very idea were ridiculous.

"He's uncomplicated," Charlie said. "Simple. Maybe that's just what she wants right now."

"I'm simple!" Theodore shot back. "I mean, who's more simple than me? I'm like a one-piece jigsaw puzzle!"

Charlie and Violet stared at him for a second, then burst into laughter.

"What?"

They kept laughing until Theodore finally joined them. It didn't get rid of all the tension, but it was a welcome break.

"I just want to say," Charlie said after they all quieted down, "that I wouldn't have made it this far without you guys. I can't explain it, exactly, but you guys mean, well, everything to me."

"I think that explains it pretty well," Violet said. "And, for the record, I feel the same way about you guys."

"Me, too," Theodore added.

Charlie turned to look out over the vast ocean.

"I don't know. Every time I try to do something good, it seems like it always turns out bad. We got the milk to save the Guardian, but that just ended up allowing Pinch to get his power back and summon the Fifth. We rescued that little kid on the 5th Ring, but that just let Slagguron escape from the Nether. We brought the Guardian to Earth, but that just ended up getting half the Nethermancers and Banishers in the Nightmare Division killed."

He shook his head.

"I try so hard to figure out what's right, and it seems like half the time it all goes wrong."

"We got a fancy word for that," a friendly voice drawled. Charlie turned to see Rex standing there with Tabitha. "We call it 'life.'"

"Hi, Rex. Hi, Tabitha," Charlie said. "I'm so glad you two are all right."

"Oh, you gotta throw more than a couple little

Nethercritters at the Princess and me to take us down."

"We're just glad you're safe," Tabitha added. "All of you."

Rex grinned. "Yeah, just think, if you'd gotten hurt, we wouldn't be able to come to this little pity party you're throwin'."

"Pity party!" Charlie exclaimed. "Come on, it's not like we're just sitting here feeling sorry for ourselves— some seriously bad stuff has happened."

"Uh-huh. Here's your problem." Rex put one dusty boot up on the lower rail of the pirate ship. "See, you think life is one plus one equals two—but it ain't. Sometimes it equals three or nineteen or a sack of magic beans. Just 'cause you do something good doesn't mean good's gonna come out of it right away. And just 'cause you do something bad doesn't mean you're gonna get punched in the kisser. But if you keep trying, and you keep making choices that are decent and moral—eventually the ball's gonna roll your way and you'll be glad you fought the fight."

"Eventually?" Charlie asked.

"Sorry, kid, I don't control the universe."

Charlie smiled. "I wish you did."

"You and me both, kid."

"Would you like a bit of good news?" Tabitha asked.

"Would we!" Violet said. "Please!"

"The Headmaster is awake . . . and she's asking for you."

The Headmaster lay on a cot in the open air of the infirmary as Mama Rose cooled her forehead with a wet cloth. Charlie didn't know the full extent of the injuries she had sustained, but she seemed weak and frail—nothing like the picture of confidence and strength that he was used to.

"I know what's happened, Mr. Benjamin," she said, her voice not much more than a whisper. "We could sit here and debate the wisdom of our previous actions if there were time, but there isn't. With the Fifth in our world, the monsters of the Nether will soon begin their assault. As you know, Pinch has betrayed us; I am in no condition to fight; and so, I'm afraid, a very dangerous and unpleasant task falls to you. You must find a way to confront the Fifth—the Ruler of the Army of the Nether—and destroy her . . . or all will be lost."

"I understand," Charlie said, not understanding at all. How could he possibly defeat something so powerful that not even the Named could stand against it?

"You will get no help from the Division, Mr. Benjamin. In fact, you must stay away from them— they will try to harm you. Nor can you stay here.

Instead, you must rely on your friends." The Headmaster nodded to Violet and Theodore. "You are very lucky to have such splendid ones."

"I agree, Headmaster."

"We won't let anything happen to him," Theodore chirped, clapping Charlie on the back. "That's a TDG—a Theodore Dagget guarantee."

"We'll do whatever it takes to protect him and get the job done," Violet added. "Don't worry."

"I won't," the Headmaster said. Then she took Charlie's hand in hers. He could feel her bones, as frail and fragile as a bird's.

"This is a task I wish had not fallen to you, Charlie," she said. "But it *has*. There will be much darkness ahead—but, in the end, there will be light."

Charlie nodded. "Yes, ma'am."

"Headmaster," Rex said, stepping up. "I'd like to take Charlie to do that 'thing' we talked about."

The Headmaster smiled weakly and nodded. "Yes. You should. He certainly deserves it."

"Come with me, kid. I think you're gonna like this. Tabitha? A portal if you please . . ."

Moments later, Charlie knocked on the door of a small apartment—it was several stories above a modest Brooklyn pizza joint called "Slice of Heaven." He heard shuffling on the other side, followed by a couple shouts of "Hold on a second! We're coming!" Finally, the door opened to reveal a tall, balding man with a kind smile and a woman with her hair done up in curlers.

They stared at Charlie in shock.

"Hi, Mom. Hi, Dad."

His mother burst into tears. "Charlie!" she screamed, grabbing him to her. She kissed him all over his cheeks, and Charlie was surprised to discover that he didn't even mind all that much.

"Son!" Barrington Benjamin exclaimed, snatching him from Olga, hugging him tightly. "My boy, we've missed you terribly!"

"I've missed you, too. So much, you wouldn't believe it."

Rex followed Charlie into the apartment and, after several slices of pizza from the place downstairs (*pretty good, actually,* Charlie thought) he found out what his parents had been up to during the six long months that they'd been hidden from him. The Nightmare Division had gotten a job for his father: "World of Batteries!" Barrington said proudly. "Anything you need to know about batteries, you just ask me!"

And his mother had busied herself with charity work at the local soup kitchen while trying to start a home bakery business.

"After smelling that delicious pizza all day long, I just couldn't resist," she explained.

Like everyone else on the planet, his parents had watched the monstrous attack at the San Diego Zoo. They were filled with questions, but Charlie was reluctant to answer them—not because he wasn't supposed to, but because, if they knew the true depth of the danger he was about to place himself in, they would worry themselves sick.

Although they're probably going to do that anyway, he thought.

"This place is nice," Charlie said, looking around at the apartment. It was far smaller than the model 3 that he'd grown up in, but his parents had made it cozy and warm and had decorated it with tons of family pictures—almost all of them of Charlie.

"It's the perfect size for us," Barrington exclaimed. "Not too big, not too little—just right, as Goldilocks would say."

Charlie smiled. Only his father would quote Goldilocks.

"So, has the Nightmare Division treated you okay?"

"Perfectly fine, Charlie," Olga replied. "They got your father his job, got us this nice apartment, and gave us new names."

"A ridiculous bit of cloak-and-dagger," Barrington

snorted. "Truth is, I like my old name just fine."

"Who are you now?"

"The Smiths," Olga replied. "Bob and Betty Smith."

Rex couldn't help but laugh. "I guess Jim and Jenny Jones must have been taken."

"I asked them the same thing!" Barrington replied. "And, you know what they said? Yes!"

Everyone laughed then. After the nightmare of the past few days, it felt good. Being around his parents seemed to Charlie almost like a dream—a wonderful dream that he wished would never end.

"What's wrong, Charlie?" his mother asked with a warm smile. "I can see it in your eyes."

"It's just . . . it's been difficult." In that moment, he seemed far older than a boy of thirteen. "See, I've done things . . . things that haven't turned out exactly the way I'd hoped."

"It doesn't matter," his mother replied simply.

"But you weren't there, Mom. I made decisions. They seemed right at the time and maybe they even *were* right, but they couldn't have ended up more wrong."

"It doesn't matter."

"Yes, but people depended on me and I let them down, and now—"

"Charlie?"

"Yes, Mom?"

"*It doesn't matter.* All that matters is that your father and I love you no matter what you do. Do you understand that? No matter what."

"Yes, Mom. I understand."

She touched his face with a warm, loving hand. "You've got so many years in front of you, Charlie. Why be in such a rush to grow up?"

He hugged her tightly, tears filling his eyes.

Rex and Charlie stood on the small balcony just off his parents' living room, surveying the bustling streets of Brooklyn far below. Multicolored twinkle lights, wrapped around the wrought-iron railing, blinked cheerfully. Inside, his parents were preparing dessert—something with chocolate and apples and thick whipped cream. It smelled delicious.

"Nice to see your folks, huh?"

"Yeah," Charlie replied. "Sure is."

"You're not gonna be alone, you know. You have your friends, and then there's Tabitha and me, of course—we'll stand by you as much as we can."

"I know. And thank you."

From down the street, they heard the sound of glass shattering, followed by another sound that Charlie had become all too familiar with:

The shriek of a Netherbat.

Then came the screaming—people shouting, horns honking. Charlie and Rex glanced at each other, saying nothing.

There was nothing to say.

"It's starting," Rex said finally.

Charlie nodded. "Yeah. I thought we'd have a little longer, but I guess we're already out of time."

The sound of sirens and the smell of smoke began to fill the night sky.

"So, you think you're ready to take on the Fifth?" Rex asked.

"No," Charlie answered honestly. "How could I be?"

"Fair enough."

They both glanced upward at the full moon, which glowed orange in the city smog. Just then, a flock of Hags flew across it, their leathery wings silhouetted against its ancient craters. They dived down into the darkness below. Terrible, gleeful cackling echoed back, followed by panicked shouts and screams.

"They do everything they can to make us fear them," Charlie said quietly. "But you know what?"

"What?"

"They should start fearing *me*." He turned to Rex

then. "I'm not a kid anymore."

"I know," the cowboy said, "and just in the nick of time, too."

He stared off into the dark, monster-filled night.

"Looks like the War of the Nether has finally begun."

NIGHTMARE ACADEMY
MONSTER
MADNESS

Excerpts from: "THE NIGHTMARE DIVISION'S
GUIDE TO THE NETHER," Including:
- A Message from Director Drake
- Bestiary

A Sneak Peek at MONSTER WAR!

3

A Message from Director Drake

Welcome, Facilitators, Banishers, and Nethermancers. My edition—the Drake edition—is to be considered the only definitive version of this guide, replacing all others, and is restricted to those Rank 3 and above. If you have not yet attained Rank 3, STOP READING IMMEDIATELY and turn yourself in to the authorities for punishment. To succeed in our endeavors, RULES MUST BE FOLLOWED and CHAOS AVOIDED!

Now that we have removed the unqualified from reading this extremely confidential document, I'd like to address a few common questions. First of all, what is the purpose of the Nightmare Division? Quite simply, our mission is to protect the citizens of Earth from the monsters of the Nether. We do this in several ways:

- We banish Nethercreatures back to the Netherworld.
- We train people who have shown an aptitude for the Gift to use it wisely or not at all, thereby preventing them from portaling monsters in the first place.
- We Reduce those who have an uncommonly powerful Gift—to stop them from mistakenly bringing the very worst of the Nethercreatures into our world (see page 212: "The Unfortunate Case of Edward Pinch and the Portalling of Verminion").

By utilizing these techniques, we seek to control the flow of monsters to our planet. Many people ask me if I am uncomfortable heading a division filled with employees who have the Gift when I do not have it myself. To them I say—how ridiculous! Does a football coach need to be on the field, getting tackled by 2,000 pounds of sweaty men, in order to call a play? Of course not!

The truth is that my lack of the Gift puts me in a perfect position to be objective. Unlike certain former directors, I do not allow myself to be swayed from the task at hand by empathizing with your difficulties. This has led some of you to accuse me of being insensitive.

You claim I don't understand how hard and often deadly your jobs are.

To that I say—NONSENSE!

I'm sure it's very tough to do the work you do . . . but do you know what else is tough? LOTS OF THINGS! Touching your nose with your tongue, for instance. Don't believe me? Try it.

My point is that the world is full of challenges that we must ALL overcome. Just because many of you have to summon your deepest, darkest fears in order to do battle with the monsters of our nightmares, please do not think that you're any stronger or better than the rest of us. Do you see me crying whenever I have to put on a tuxedo to attend a champagne dinner or write an order to have someone Reduced? Of course not!

Now that we're all on the same page, I invite you

to dive into this extensively researched and incredibly useful guidebook. Inside you will find a Map of the Nether; a Bestiary of many of the Monsters of the Nether (see page 86 for detailed information on the greatly overrated Trout of Truth); a glossary to help you understand commonly used terms (e.g., Wetwash, Portal Barricade); a history of our Allies in the Nether (see pages 147–154 for great detail about our special relationship with the Guardian and pages 182–189 to learn much about the NetherForge and its ruler, the Smith).

And that's just the tip of the proverbial iceberg.

Keep this guidebook handy.

Keep it safe.

Keep it away from those who would do us harm.

Sincerely,

Reginald Drake

Director of the Nightmare Division

Bestiary

Netherbat

Description: The leathery skin of these giant bats is most often crimson, although they can come in virtually any color. Their wingspan is much wider than those of terrestrial bats, and their long front fangs are hollowed out (like a snake's) for use in draining a victim's blood.

Class: Determined by size.

Class 1's are roughly equivalent to the length of a large dog (e.g., German shepherd). By the time they achieve full Class 5 status, they can be as big as an airplane.

Note: Tyrannus (one of the four Lords of the Nether) is, by most accounts, an immense and fierce Netherbat. For more information on him and the other Lords of the Nether, refer to "Lords of the Netherworld: What You Need to Know" (pages 144–168).

Combat Tactics: Netherbats typically kill by grabbing their prey with their strong front talons, carrying it high into the air, and then dropping it from a great height. If attacked by a Netherbat, it is IMPERATIVE to fight the monster on the ground. If allowed to carry you into the air, the Netherbat WILL drop you to your death. At that point, aside from the occasional miracle, only Nethermancers have a shot at survival by performing the extremely difficult Portal Cushion maneuver (see page 211 for more

EXTRAS

information on the advanced Portal Cushion).

Do not rely on it!

Note: In close quarters, the fierce wind created by the flapping of a Netherbat's wings has been known to knock even the strongest Banisher off his or her feet. Be wary.

Weaknesses: Netherbats, like regular bats, rely on a specialized form of sonar called echolocation in order to "see." Very small particles (e.g., flour, talcum powder) can be used to clog their transmitters, effectively rendering them blind. For this reason, it is advisable to carry a bag of flour wherever you are likely to encounter this particular monster.

Netherleapers

Description: Netherleapers are carnivorous, kangaroolike creatures, often referred to (incorrectly) as Dangeroos. They are one of the few monsters of the Nether to roam in herds (see GREMLINS, pages 192–193). Their forelimbs are much stronger than a terrestrial kangaroo's, and their great hind legs provide them with massive pouncing power. Netherleaper jumps as high as one hundred yards have been reported.

Class: Determined by length of fang.

Although they grow in size as they rise in class (the largest could comfortably fit a grown man into their front pouches—see below), the formal ranking is determined by the length of the fangs. A Class 1 Netherleaper has 1-inch fangs, a Class 2 has 2-inch fangs, etc.

Combat Tactics: Netherleapers prefer to disorient their prey, making them easier to consume. This is normally achieved in three steps:

1) They utilize their horrific stink (famously referred to as "skunk, mixed with hot garbage, blended in the butt-end of a sewer"—Rexford Henderson, Banisher 5th Rank) to dramatically weaken their intended food source.

2) They then grab their prey with their forelimbs and stuff it into their front pouch, immobilizing it. The lack of oxygen coupled with their terrible smell is said to create a "dazelike" feeling.

3) Once their prey is firmly secured in their pouch, they leap up and down, hundreds of feet into the air, for several minutes. Few people are able to quickly shake off the dizzying effect of these jumps.

These three factors—the smell, the lack of oxygen, and the breathless leaps and drops—combine to disorient the Netherleaper's prey so completely that most people are able to offer no resistance when the monster finally decides to feed.

Weaknesses: Netherleapers rely on wide-open spaces to perform their astonishing jumps. A contained

Netherleaper, denied the opportunity to rocket into the air, is a crippled Netherleaper. Choice of venue for a fight with this monster is CRITICAL.

Ravenous Sticky-Spitters

Description: These large, lizardlike creatures are unique in their ability to change the pigment in their skin to mirror whatever is directly behind them, making them incredibly hard to see. As difficult as it is to spot a mature Ravenous Sticky-Spitter on the move (they are often referred to as "a blur") identifying one at rest is nearly impossible, given how completely the monster can blend into its surroundings.

Class: Determined by camouflage ability.

Because their ability to blend into their surroundings is the only reliable way to determine the class of a Ravenous Sticky-Spitter, ranking them can be difficult. A poorly disguised Ravenous Sticky-Spitter is likely to be a Class 1 or 2. A Ravenous Sticky-Spitter that you cannot see is likely to be a Class 4 or 5.

Combat Tactics: Ravenous Sticky-Spitters are so named for their ability to spit from their mouths a clear, gummy substance that coats their fleeing prey, gluing it to the ground. Because they prefer to consume their prey alive, their spit is always carefully aimed to avoid covering the victim's face, where it would likely suffocate the victim. Although done for a gruesome purpose, this technique gives the intended victim a few extra moments to attempt an escape.

Weaknesses: Fortunately the sticky phlegm of the Ravenous Sticky-Spitter can be melted by the purple Netherflames that blossom during portalling. Unfortunately Banishers have no such means of escape and are, consequently, much weaker against these fiendish foes. This explains the derivation of the cliché: "Dead as a Banisher fighting a Sticky-Spitter."

CHARLIE BENJAMIN AND HIS FRIENDS CONTINUE THE
FIGHT AGAINST THE ARMY OF THE NETHER IN . . .

NIGHTMARE ACADEMY
MONSTER WAR

BOOK 3

MONSTERS AT THE MALL

Three Netherbats crashed through the large front window of the McDonald's. The crimson beasts sailed inside with a terrible shriek, furiously flapping their leathery wings as customers dove for cover to escape the blinding spray of glass.

Charlie reached under his booth. "Well, I may not be able to get rid of all the monsters in the world—but I can sure get rid of *these*."

He stood, now holding his glowing blue rapier firmly in hand.

EXTRAS

Just one week earlier, the thought of carrying a weapon in public, even a relatively harmless one like a rapier, would have seemed absurd—but the monster invasion had changed all that. People began to arm themselves even as they irrationally tried to continue going about their daily business as if nothing truly unusual was happening—as if flocks of Hags swooping out of a nighttime sky to snatch entire football teams from their stadiums (the starting lineup of the Dallas Cowboys was the most recent casualty) was just another hazard of modern daily life.

"Help! It's got me!" a man by the cash registers screamed as one of the Netherbats wrapped its knotty claws around his chest, partially obscuring the slogan written across his stretched T-shirt: "Kiss Me—I Don't Bite."

Mr. Kiss Me I Don't Bite shrieked shrilly as the monster spun around and flapped toward the shattered window, trying to escape with its flailing prize.

It didn't get far.

With one quick, smooth move, Charlie leaped into the air and brought his sizzling rapier down on the beast's left wing. The sliced appendage fell to the ground in a fountain of black ichor, and the Netherbat, off balance now, careened into the condiment counter in a goopy explosion of mustard and ketchup. Still flapping with its one remaining wing, it flipped onto its back and slammed into the restaurant wall. The nearby customers scrambled to crawl away as the beast snapped at them until Charlie put a quick stop to that by chopping off its head.

"Th-thank you!" the man exclaimed, but before Charlie could even mutter "You're welcome," he turned to the remaining two Netherbats cruising the store for tasty human prey. Charlie gutted one of the beasts as it soared over his head and then quickly dispatched the other as it flew into the kitchen. The beast's carcass slammed down onto the grill, where it cooked and sizzled alongside the burger patties and fried onions.

There was silence then and the only sound Charlie heard was the popping of frying meat. After a moment it was joined by another sound.

Clapping.

Charlie turned to see the customers in the restaurant applauding as they struggled to their feet. "Me?" he whispered. Were they clapping for him?

Suddenly he heard screaming. Through one of the side windows of the McDonald's, he saw a mass of people rushing out of the nearby mall.

Something had gotten inside.

Something *bad*.

Fleeing customers flooded from the entrance in waves, and pushing through them was like trying to break through heavy surf; but somehow Charlie managed. Once inside, he tried to distance himself from the screams and cries of the panicked people around him to figure out the *cause* of their terror. His first clue came from a woman just outside a Banana Republic. People streamed past her, but for some reason this woman wasn't moving.

That's strange, Charlie thought. And then he realized *why*.

She was covered, from the neck down, in a clear, gummy mass that completely immobilized her, anchoring her to the floor. Charlie glanced around and saw that she wasn't the only one encased in the gluey mess—a security guard in the food court on the second story was trapped against the cash register of a China Bowl restaurant, and two kids in the play area were stuck to a giant, foam ladybug.

Only one monster does that, Charlie thought, looking around frantically. And then he saw it:

A Ravenous Sticky-Spitter.

The large lizardlike creature clung to the outside of a glass elevator that was moving down from the third floor to the first. The beast was incredibly hard to spot—Sticky-Spitters had terrific camouflage; the pigment in their skin mirrored their surroundings so perfectly that most people could see them only when they moved. Charlie couldn't recall ever having come into contact with one before, but that didn't mean he hadn't—one could have been sleeping in the bed next to him without his ever seeing it.

As the elevator landed on the first floor, the Sticky-Spitter opened its wide mouth and spat out a large wad of glistening goop that shot through the air and snagged a fleeing worker from the Foot Locker. It knocked him into the window of a Hallmark Card Shop and stuck him there.

At least his face isn't covered, Charlie noted. He knew from class that Ravenous Sticky-Spitters preferred to swallow their food alive, so they carefully aimed their spit to immobilize their prey, not suffocate it.

With his rapier glowing fiercely blue, Charlie rushed toward the Sticky-Spitter with the unnatural speed and grace of a born Banisher, weaving through fleeing customers like a matador dodging a rush of oncoming bulls. But as fast as Charlie was, he wasn't faster than the gluey phlegm that the Sticky-Spitter hurled his way and, before he even knew what was happening, he found himself stuck to the floor of the mall as surely as a fly to flypaper.